Seven Sins

One man's betrayal can destroy generations.

Fifteen years ago, a hedge-fund hotshot vanished with billions, leaving the high-powered families of Falling Brook changed forever.

Now seven heirs, shaped by his betrayal, must reckon with the sins of the past.

Passion may be their only path to redemption.

Experience all Seven Sins!

* * *

Ruthless Pride by **Naima Simone**

This CEO's pride led him to give up his dreams
for his family. Now he's drawn to the woman
who threatens everything...

Forbidden Lust by **Karen Booth**

He's always resisted his lust for his best friend's sister—
until they're stranded together in paradise...

Insatiable Hunger by **Yahrah St. John**

His unbridled appetite for his closest friend is unleashed
when he believes she's fallen for the wrong man...

Hidden Ambition by **Jules Bennett**

Ambition has taken him far, but revenge could
cost him his one chance at love...

Reckless Envy by **Joss Wood**

When this shark in the boardroom meets the one
woman he can't have, envy takes over...

Untamed Passion by **Cat Schield**

Will this black sheep's self-destructive wrath flame
out when he's expecting an heir of his own?

Slow Burn by **Janice Maynard**

If he's really the idle playboy his family claims, will his
inaction threaten a reunion with the woman who got away?

"So what's your angle here?" she asked Chase.

"You want the CEO position so bad that you're willing to fake date me? Or is there something else you're after?"

His eyes darkened as they dropped to her lips.

"Oh, there are several things I want, Haley."

Haley leaned in closer and murmured, "Sex isn't on the table."

"No?"

"I'm going to figure out your angle. I can't believe you're going through all of this just to land a position at Black Crescent."

He eased over on the bench, his arm sliding even farther behind her back as he bent closer to her face. Those eyes once again dropped to her mouth and she couldn't stop that knee-jerk reaction of licking her lips.

Anticipation soared through her. Is this when he'd kiss her?

"Maybe I'm trying to land you," he murmured against her lips.

* * *

Hidden Ambition by Jules Bennett is part of the Dynasties: Seven Sins series.

JULES BENNETT

HIDDEN AMBITION

HARLEQUIN

DESIRE_t

To my girls, Grace and Madelyn. Thanks for keeping things running while I was pressed for time with this deadline. You two are my world.

Special thanks and acknowledgment are given to Jules Bennett for her contribution to the Dynasties: Seven Sins miniseries.

DESIRE

Recycling programs for this product may not exist in your area.

ISBN-13: 978-1-335-20926-9

Hidden Ambition

Harlequin Enterprises ULC
22 Adelaide St. West, 40th Floor
Toronto, Ontario M5H 4E3, Canada
www.Harlequin.com

Dear Reader,

Are you loving the Seven Sins series? I was thrilled to be asked to contribute! The minute I received the plot for *Hidden Ambition*, I couldn't wait to get started. Chase and Haley were so fun to write with that cat and mouse game they played. These strong characters knew what they wanted and were determined to stop at nothing to reach their goals!

While Chase might seem a little sneaky, I do hope you'll forgive him as he was only trying to protect his family and seek justice—he just started about it all the wrong way.

There are so many secrets to still be revealed, so sit back and relax. This Seven Sins ride is far from over! I present to you...*greed*!

Happy reading,

Jules

USA TODAY bestselling author **Jules Bennett** has published over sixty books and never tires of writing happy endings. Writing strong heroines and alpha heroes is Jules's favorite way to spend her workdays. Jules hosts weekly contests on her Facebook fan page and loves chatting with readers on Twitter, Facebook and via email through her website. Stay up-to-date by signing up for her newsletter at julesbennett.com.

Books by Jules Bennett

Harlequin Desire

The Rancher's Heirs

Twin Secrets
Claimed by the Rancher
Taming the Texan
A Texan for Christmas

Two Brothers

Montana Seduction
California Secrets

Lockwood Lightning

An Unexpected Scandal
Scandalous Engagement

Dynasties: Seven Sins

Hidden Ambition

Visit her Author Profile page at Harlequin.com, or julesbennett.com, for more titles.

You can also find Jules Bennett on Facebook, along with other Harlequin Desire authors, at Facebook.com/harlequindesireauthors!

One

Haley Shaw bent over the gift boxes, searching around the obscene bouquets of flowers and cupcake boxes, just trying to find her damn yellow highlighter.

"That's quite a display."

The low, throaty voice was all too familiar... and all too arousing.

Haley straightened and turned to face a smirking, sexy Chase Hargrove. The persistent man was vying for the coveted position of CEO of Black Crescent Hedge Fund. The successful investment firm had been through hell and back, and Haley had stuck through it all—which made her the target of all the résumés and all of the bribes. Hence the gifts cluttering her normally pristine work space.

"I assume you were referring to the flowers and boxes and not the fact I was bent over with my backside facing you while looking for my highlighter," she stated, smoothing down her conservative dove-gray pencil dress.

His deep brown eyes held hers. "Of course."

Sure. That naughty grin gave him away and she had a feeling a powerful man like Chase always held his emotions and cards close to his chest. He wanted her unnerved, thrown off track. Well, it would take a hell of a lot more than charm and a little flirting to really get her attention.

Haley prided herself on her professionalism. She'd worked too hard, overcome too much, to land where she was. True, she was an executive assistant, but she had power here at Black Crescent and she never let her emotions, or a man, get in the way of her duties.

Not even this sexy man who was very qualified to take over the coveted CEO position and potentially become her boss.

"Do you have an appointment?" she asked, knowing full well he didn't.

Chase had been popping in and out over the

past several weeks, ever since Josh Lowell had announced he was stepping down and the CEO position would be available. Chase had turned in a rather impressive résumé and had even landed an interview a few weeks ago. The position had been offered to Ryan Hathaway, but ultimately, Ryan turned down the coveted title. So the search continued as Chase moved closer to the top of the list. Hence Chase pursuing the job…and her.

Not that she minded a sexy distraction, but she really did need to get her work done and there was no chance of that as long as Chase stood at her desk with that panty-dropping stare.

Maybe he really was here for the job, but he spent an exorbitant amount of time charming her.

Haley was Josh's right-hand woman and everyone thought she was the gatekeeper in regards to the top position. Haley had to admit, she didn't hate all of this attention. Who could be mad when cupcakes, flowers and chocolates were delivered on the daily?

"I do have an appointment," he amended with a naughty, crooked grin. "With you."

Confused, she crossed her arms over her chest. "Me?"

"For lunch."

Oh, he was a smooth one. He thought he could waltz in here, pour on the charisma and she'd just take him up on a day date? Clearly he knew nothing about women…or at least this woman. She didn't let anything interrupt her work. Or at least, she never did before him.

"I'm not free for lunch." She lifted one vase, then another, on her desk, glancing for all the things she'd lost in this chaos. "But you go have a nice time."

"What are you looking for?" he asked, obviously in no hurry to go.

"My highlighter," she informed him. "I keep getting all of these gifts and I've run out of room for things I actually need. I normally have everything in a designated spot, but now…"

She tossed her hands up, frustrated with how quickly her space had become unorganized.

"When we go to lunch, we can stop and get you as many new highlighters as you need," he suggested. "My treat."

Haley glanced up and really wished her belly would stop doing those schoolgirl flops over a hot guy and his offer to buy her dollar markers.

So what if his shoulders perfectly filled out that black suit jacket? So what if his messy hair looked like he'd just rolled out of his lover's bed? He wouldn't be rolling out of her bed, so she really had no place fantasizing about such things.

She had important issues to tend to and getting

distracted by a man who likely wasn't interested in her, but in how far she could get him in this field, was not one of them.

The phone on her desk rang and she sighed. "If you'll excuse me, I need to get back to work."

She took the call and moments later when she hung up, she was surprised to see he had actually left. But there wasn't a doubt in her mind that Chase Hargrove would be back. A man like that never gave up.

Chase clutched the surprise in his hand and headed into Black Crescent Hedge Fund for the second time that morning. Determination and revenge were a combination that no rejection could penetrate.

No matter how many times he had to show his face, flirt a little or buy silly bribes, he'd sure as hell do it. A little humility was nothing in comparison with what his family had gone through at the hands of Vernon Lowell.

The sneaky bastard had squandered millions and disappeared fifteen years ago, but Chase would never forget the struggle his family went through after his father was framed by Vernon to take some of the fall.

Chase's father had landed in prison for a few years, paying for his actions after Vernon had left a neat and tidy paper trail leading right to their door.

Now Chase had the opportunity to seek his own justice, since Vernon was never caught. His son Josh was now at the helm, and Chase didn't find him exempt from the damage.

He hadn't counted on the perks of the revenge plot, though. Getting an eyeful of Haley Shaw was certainly an added bonus. There was something about her unruffled attitude that made him want to just get his digs in where he could…which was why he didn't mind one bit that she'd caught him staring at her ass.

He wasn't a jerk or a guy who took advantage of women. He respected women, but if a male held the position that Haley did, Chase would certainly be going about this via a much different route.

As he stepped through the double glass doors, he nodded to the receptionist and headed toward the elevators. One day soon, this would all be his. Chase had the credentials and was more than qualified to settle perfectly into the CEO position. But if not, then he'd at least get the scoop he needed to help bring Black Crescent down for good. They deserved nothing less and Haley was inadvertently going to help him.

As for the top slot here, Chase didn't need it. He sure as hell wasn't hurting for money, but he wouldn't mind adding another investment firm to his portfolio.

Chase stepped out of the elevator and walked toward Haley's large circular desk, and once again the overwhelming scent of flowers assaulted him. He shouldn't be surprised at all the candidates vying for her attention, though they were being too predictable. Boxes of gourmet chocolates? Oversize floral arrangements? Cupcakes from the local bakery? Please. Those candidates were amateurs and utterly boring.

Haley had her back to him and was holding a stack of papers, muttering beneath her breath. A woman getting caught up in her work was damn sexy, but he wasn't here for seduction. Shame that. Having Haley under different circumstances wasn't something he'd turn down. Classy, smart, powerful… She was the entire package of sex appeal.

Chase pushed lustful thoughts from his head and tapped his knuckles on the edge of the desk. She startled and glanced over her shoulder, her wavy blond hair framing her face.

"Back so soon?" she asked, quirking a brow.

Damn if her sarcasm didn't up his attraction to her. He had to admit, this challenge wasn't proving to be boring. He actually looked forward to his interactions with Haley.

Chase held up the present. "I brought you something."

Her eyes darted to his hand and she turned fully to face him. "Seriously?" She laughed as she circled her desk. "Is that a bouquet of highlighters?"

He extended the gift. "You couldn't find yours and you had enough flowers and gourmet-cupcake boxes."

She stared at the bundle for a second before she took the variety of colors. The wide smile on her face was like a punch of lust to his gut. Not exactly what he'd come looking for, but something about her simple style and natural beauty appealed to a side he didn't want to be appealed to.

Lust and desire didn't follow guidelines, though. He couldn't help this attraction and he couldn't help but wonder if she was getting that kick of arousal, as well.

"Well done," she told him with a wide grin. "I admire someone who thinks outside the box."

Chase shoved his hands in his pockets. "Admire enough to go to lunch? You do get a lunch break, right?"

"I do," she confirmed. "But I'm not going to lunch with you. I have other plans."

"Cancel them."

She cocked her head. "Are you always demanding?"

"When I see something I want."

And there it was. A glimpse of desire he hadn't

quite been sure about flashed through her eyes. Well, well, well. Maybe he could keep working this angle and come out with the job and a side fling. Win-win.

"Fine," she conceded. "We'll go to lunch, but we will not talk business."

Not talk business? No problem. He could gather information from her without her even realizing he was doing so. He hadn't gotten this far making billions by not being able to read people.

Besides, he'd already worn her down—by a bouquet of highlighters, no less. Chase was confident he would get damaging intel from her and she wouldn't have a clue she'd even let him in.

"Lead the way," he said, gesturing to her door.

Chase followed those swaying hips and reminded himself he was here for a purpose, a vendetta, not to see how quickly he could slide that zipper down and have her out of that body-hugging dress.

Only time would tell which one of them came out on top... But Chase didn't intend to lose.

Two

Haley nodded her thanks to the concierge as he opened the door for her and Chase. The posh, up-scale restaurant was a bit over-the-top for a lunch between virtual strangers, but this was where he'd chosen and she actually did love their Mediterranean salad.

"Welcome back, Mr. Hargrove," the hostess promptly greeted them with all smiles. "I have your usual table all set up."

Haley bit the inside of her cheek to keep quiet as she followed the hostess back to the corner of the restaurant. The intimate table for two offered a spectacular view of New York City, one she appreciated when she ate here at night.

Once they were seated and alone, Haley glanced across the table. "So, how many women do you bring here, Mr. Hargrove?"

"Chase," he corrected with a crooked grin. "And not many."

"Yet you have a usual table and I can't imagine a man like you eating alone." She pulled in a breath and leveled her gaze. "Chase."

His eyes dropped to her lips the second she said his name and she seriously wished she would've kept the *Mr. Hargrove* in the conversation. It wasn't like her to get all tingly at the sight of a man, but no man had looked at her like he wanted to devour her...at least not in a long time.

Maybe she needed to date. Perhaps she'd been working too much. Once this new CEO position was filled, she would work on her social life. But not with a man like Chase Hargrove.

Chase was a man who no doubt liked nice things, always had a sexy woman on his arm and demanded people to bow to him. She'd seen enough of his type over the years in this business to know exactly what he required. She was most definitely not his type.

No, Chase flirted and was no doubt going to all this trouble to get into that top slot at Black

Crescent. She wasn't stupid, but she'd let him play his little game if that made him feel better about himself.

And, hey, she got new highlighters and a lunch out of it, so this wasn't a total loss. Besides, the view across the table was rather appetizing.

"I'm confident enough to eat alone," he replied. "I often meet acquaintances here or friends and, yes, I have brought a date here a time or two."

"And what category are you sliding me into?" she asked, smoothing the cloth napkin onto her lap.

Those dark eyes shielded by heavy lids could make a woman forget whom she was dealing with. But Haley wasn't a ditz, despite how she'd been treated for years by her family.

She'd fought damn hard to get where she was today, with no help from her parents. Being an executive assistant wasn't easy work and oftentimes could be overlooked considering the amount of behind-the-scenes tasks that were involved. That wasn't the case with working with Josh. They clashed every now and then, but they also had a mutual respect for each other.

And now they were working closely together to find the perfect replacement to take Black Crescent into a successful, prosperous future.

Haley prided herself on how loyal and dedicated she had been to a company that had floundered amid the biggest scandal this town had ever seen and had climbed back up out of the ashes.

True, she may have gone only to a community college, but that didn't make her degree any less important or inferior to her brother's Ivy League status.

"Which category do you want to be in?" he retorted.

Pulling herself back into the moment, Haley pursed her lips and weighed her answer, but thankfully the waiter came by. Of course Chase knew the man by name, asked about his work, made a joke and laughed. This must be a favorite hot spot for Chase...or the man owned the place.

Josh trusted her to see things he didn't. Allison Randall, the executive recruiter Black Crescent hired, did the professional vetting on his résumé. Everything was perfect.

Too perfect? Haley made a mental note to dig into Chase's past and find out just what he was up to. Of course, he'd had a remarkable résumé and all of his references had checked out, but she wanted to know more. She wanted to dive into that personal side of him that he hadn't revealed.

Haley didn't believe he'd go to all this trouble just to be the CEO of Black Crescent. And she certainly didn't believe he was trying to sway her into dating him—maybe bed her.

Haley and Chase both placed their drink orders and sent the waiter away. Before they could circle back to the conversation, her cell chimed and she slid the phone from her purse. One glance to the screen and she sent Chase an apologetic smile.

"I need to take this," she told him.

Chase nodded. "I understand. Business first."

But it wasn't the business he was thinking and she didn't necessarily need privacy, so she eased back in her seat and answered.

"Marcus," she greeted. "I was going to call you this afternoon."

"I just wanted to touch base with you regarding the latest funding," her right-hand man told her. "The latest investor doubled their original donation."

Haley gasped. "You're serious?"

She didn't miss the way Chase stared at her, hanging on every word. This call had nothing to do with Black Crescent and everything to do with Haley's charity that was like her baby.

"Very," Marcus replied. "That means we can take on seven more high school seniors."

Haley closed her eyes and pulled in a deep breath, relieved they could take on more teens in need. This was the best news. She'd been struggling to get to the stack of applicants from area high schools.

Her nonprofit, Tomorrow's Leaders, aided teens who wouldn't be able to go to college without the funding of an outside source. Not every kid wanted a student loan they'd have to pay back before some even found a job. These underprivileged kids deserved the best opportunity for a solid foundation to jump-start their futures and Haley was all too happy to make it happen.

She had been that underprivileged kid. Her parents had put her older brother through Harvard, but that had sucked up their entire savings. They'd believed he would become some master surgeon or celebrity attorney… Hell, she didn't know what their plans had been. All Haley knew was they had low expectations for her and no money to expand her education beyond high school. So Haley had worked her ass off to pay for the community schooling and graduated top of her class without any outside help.

"I will take this evening and look through the files again," she told Marcus. "I can't tell you what a blessing this is to know we can take on more kids."

"I knew you'd be thrilled. That's why I wanted to call and not text. I hope I didn't interrupt anything."

Her eyes met Chase's again and he didn't even bother to hide the fact he was staring.

"Your timing was just fine," she stated. "I'll get back with you late tonight or early tomorrow about the applicants."

Haley disconnected the call and slid the phone back into her purse.

"Kids?" he asked, raising his brows.

She smiled. "Well, teenagers, but considering I'm thirty-four, they're kids to me."

"You work with teens?" he asked, clearly shocked, and if she was reading him right, maybe a little impressed.

"For several years now," she confirmed, proud of the work she'd done all on her own. "I run Tomorrow's Leaders. It's a nonprofit organization that assists college-aged students who wouldn't otherwise be able to go. Not everyone wants the black cloud of student loans looming over them when they graduate, and many kids can't afford to further their education and they aren't all eligible for scholarships."

Chase listened, his eyes never wavering from hers. Not everyone knew what she did in her spare time. Not that she wasn't extremely proud of the work she'd done, but she wasn't one to brag and she didn't really have the time to socialize between finding a new CEO and running her charity.

"Impressive," he stated as he leaned back in his chair. "You're one busy woman."

"Which is why I often eat lunch at my desk," she informed him.

"Then I'm doubly glad I got you out of there."

Chase smiled, which really shouldn't make her belly do flops, but the man was a little more potent than she'd first given him credit for. She had to remain on her toes where this one was concerned.

"How long have you been doing this nonprofit?" he asked.

Haley never tired of talking about her cause. She didn't talk to many outside of her office or those directly involved with Tomorrow's Leaders. Her family didn't even know what she did, but then again, she rarely saw or spoke to them.

But who knew, maybe Chase would want to become a donor.

"Twelve years," she informed him. "As soon as I finished school, I started campaigning for donors and working to get something up and running. The first year, I was only able to help one guy, but that was better than nothing. Even if I could only help one person a year, I would still fight just as hard for funding."

Chase stared across the table, then leaned forward, resting his forearms on the white cloth. "What makes you so vigilant about this subject? You went to college, right?"

"I did," she confirmed. "But my backstory is not up for discussion."

Discussing her whys for the whole nonprofit organization wasn't her favorite topic, and the last thing she ever wanted was for someone to believe she felt sorry for herself. She didn't pity her childhood or how she managed to make it through college. If she didn't have those hardships, she wouldn't be the strong career woman she was today and she wouldn't have founded Tomorrow's Leaders. Maybe her parents hadn't done her a disservice after all.

Added to all of that, Chase was still out for his own gains and she didn't want to give him any insight to her personal life. This was nothing more than a lunch between strangers. If he was trying to seduce her, well, that was a whole other level of consideration for her to think about.

"Maybe on our second date," he stated with a grin.

Haley laughed. "This isn't a date."

"No? Well, then we'll have to fix that." He curled his hand around his water glass and tipped his head. "Friday at eight. I'll send a car to pick you up."

Haley stared at him for a moment before she busted out laughing. "Does that usually work for you? Just to demand like that?"

He shrugged. "Do you have other plans?"

"My personal life really isn't your concern," she replied.

"And yet you shared your nonprofit with me and had such compassion in your tone," he retorted. "I'd say that's pretty personal."

"Maybe I was hoping you'd want to donate."

His lips twitched and she knew he was biting back a smile. Good. He needed to keep those sexy smiles to a minimum for her sanity.

"One hundred thousand dollars."

"Excuse me?" she asked.

"I'll give Tomorrow's Leaders one hundred thousand dollars if you go out with me on Friday."

Haley narrowed her eyes, disappointed he'd resorted to buying her. "I can't be bought, not even for my foundation."

Obviously he wasn't used to taking no for an answer, but he might as well get used to it because she was not giving in. Okay, the highlighters had won him a lunch, but no more.

They placed their orders and Haley really wished she would've stayed in her office for lunch like always. She had too much to do, too many things to oversee, and she honestly hated leaving in the middle of a workday.

Being so valuable within Black Crescent made her feel a sense of worth, one she hadn't found with anything else in her life. She'd come there as an intern straight out of college and had only grown with each passing year. There were secrets she knew that she would never reveal, and that was why Josh Lowell entrusted her with the daunting task of helping him find his replacement.

Because she was the longest-standing employee, résumés were sent to her and not to Josh, or even to Allison Randall, the executive recruiter.

Haley and Josh had both laughed about the fact people were wanting to deal with her, because she wasn't the final decision maker. Although, she rather enjoyed knowing how powerful some people thought she was.

Her cell chimed again and she didn't even apologize for taking this next call. After Chase had offered a ridiculous amount to take her on a real date, she didn't care what he thought or if her manners were lacking.

Josh's name lit up her screen and she slid her finger across to answer.

"Hey, Josh."

"Haley, sorry to interrupt your lunch. I just had a quick question."

"No problem at all."

The waiter came with their food and Chase made work of cutting up his chicken, but she knew he was hanging on every word.

"I can't find Matt's résumé," he began. "I had it before his first interview and I wanted to look at it again."

The names slid through her mind, but Matteo Velez stood out. Matt's résumé was impeccable and he'd aced the first interview.

"I still have it on my computer," she told her boss. "I'll get it to you as soon as I get back."

"I ran into him the other evening when I was out with Sophie," Josh told her. "He bought my dinner, actually."

Josh chuckled, but Haley rolled her eyes. Everyone thought they could get ahead by buying their way, but that didn't fly with her. She'd rather have actions, not money being tossed around.

A lesson Chase would do well to learn.

"Please remember, I'm going to need someone personable I can get along with once you're gone and I don't know Matt too well."

"I promise not to leave you with a bastard," Josh stated. "Get me his résumé when you can. With Ryan out of the running, I just want to look closer at Matt. He did seem like a nice guy, and that was before I found out he bought my dinner."

"I'll be back in thirty minutes and I'll get it right to you."

"I knew I could count on you," he stated before hanging up.

Haley really did dread the day when Josh would leave. He'd been an upstanding boss and she'd come to think of him as a friend. But he wanted to start a new chapter in his life and she really couldn't blame him.

After the scandal with his father disappearing and pilfering millions from clients, Josh had rebuilt Black Crescent Hedge Fund. His twin, Jake, had wanted nothing to do with the family business and had taken off for Europe. And their youngest brother, Oliver, had his own issues, namely being a recovering addict and professional partier. He had his own mess of a reputation to overcome, and stepping into the top role of a tarnished hedge-fund company was not a position he was ready for.

So, Josh stepped up and Haley had been right there by his side, helping him rebuild. People who went through hell together shared a special bond. It would take one very exceptional man or woman to replace someone as strong and resilient as Josh Lowell.

"Sounds like the hunt is still on," Chase casually mentioned as he pierced a baby potato with his fork. "I imagine you and Josh are having a difficult time narrowing down a potential replacement."

"No work talk," she reminded him with a smile. "But if you want to talk business, you can tell me what exactly you do. I want to know what's not on your résumé."

"Eager to learn more about me?" he asked with a mischievous grin. "I deal with investments, but I also travel and help other companies across the globe work on strengthening their own firms."

Which sounded like the perfect replacement for Josh. But Chase would have to have more than the perfect answer to get the position, and this certainly wasn't an interview.

"Are you from here?" she asked.

"Born and raised about twenty minutes away," he told her. "My father was also an investor and my mother was a stay-at-home mom. I'm an only child. Nothing much to tell, really. I went to college on a full-ride football scholarship. My parents struggled a bit, so I'm not sure we could've afforded it otherwise."

That would explain that broad frame and she could easily see him in the role of a star athlete. She also wouldn't mind seeing him in those tight pants.

Focus, Haley. You don't even like football.

Haley was surprised at how similar they were in fighting for what they wanted and being so headstrong, but she wasn't going to admit any such thing. Chase was clearly looking for that edge up and she certainly wasn't going to just hand him the ammunition.

All of her attraction aside, Josh had the final say over the new CEO, and Haley wasn't so sure being sexually drawn to your new boss was the best position to be in.

"I have updated my résumé since my first interview," he went on. "You have a new copy in your inbox."

Shocked, she set her fork down and dabbed her mouth with her napkin. "And when did you resend?"

"Right before I came back with your gift," he explained. "I rebuilt a multibillion-dollar firm in Europe and I included those stats and references. They'll all give me a glowing recommendation, by the way."

Damn it. He was getting more qualified by the moment.

Haley instantly had a vision of working with him day in and day out. She'd been side by side with Josh for years now and never once had she been attracted to him, not in the intimate way. He was certainly a handsome man, but she'd never gotten those giddy feelings…nothing like with Chase, and she'd only been with him for an hour.

Giddy? No. Almost arousing, which was even more dangerous.

Yeah, working with Chase Hargrove for hours on end would be a mistake. No doubt he would continue to try to wear her down.

Good thing she was on to him.

Three

Chase felt confident about his lunch date with Haley. Flirting came easy and he'd actually found himself caught up in her beauty, and suddenly charming her didn't seem to be a chore.

He'd been stunned to learn of her charity work. That someone with a demanding career spent her spare time helping those less fortunate was a hell of a turn-on…and quite a juxtaposition to how the Lowells were.

Sure Joshua gave money here and there, probably guilt money, but the Lowells still held themselves up on another pedestal, towering above everybody else.

Chase stood in his living room and stared out the wall of one-way windows overlooking the river. The lights from Falling Brook sparkled against the darkened sky and calmed him. Though his mind continued to race, he at least felt peace about where he was heading.

Plotting and planning had gotten him to where he was today. Being a prominent international investor gave him an obvious edge up to slide into the CEO position at Black Crescent Hedge Fund. Not that he cared about that position. He wanted information to bring the company and the Lowell family down once and for all.

He'd seen his parents struggle after all of their savings were lost. His father had gone to prison for fraud thanks to Vernon's antics, and those attorney's fees hadn't come cheap. His mother had ultimately suffered a nervous breakdown and had needed medical attention. Nothing motivated Chase more than someone harming those he loved. His parents were doing so much better now, but that heaviness still hovered over them. They certainly weren't the same, but they were still a strong family and still pushing through each day to be their best.

Chase needed to continue to get closer to Haley. She'd thrown him off his game for a moment when she'd started discussing her charity. How did she find time to run such a thing when she was always at Black Crescent? Her job as executive assistant was demanding and he knew she put her entire heart and soul into that position. If the woman never even took a lunch break, that was loyalty and dedication on another level.

Did Josh demand that type of work or was that all Haley wanting to go above and beyond?

Clearly she didn't have much of a social life between the two full-time jobs vying for her attention. He made a mental note to check into Tomorrow's Leaders and find out all he could about what sounded like a brilliant charity. Whether she agreed to a date or not, he would make a sizable contribution because he loved the concept. He would do so anonymously so she didn't think he was literally trying to buy her affection. He wasn't that much of a bastard. That's something the Lowell family would do to get attention and make gains.

But Haley would agree to a date with him, with or without the monetary help. He wouldn't mention the donation again, because that had been a little shady. The words had slipped out before he could think better of it and he'd immediately regretted putting her in that position or making her feel like she was nothing more than a bribe.

Just because he'd charmed her into lunch didn't

mean he would be able to go that route again. No. Someone like Haley needed to be kept on her toes and surprised. He didn't miss the way she smiled and was actually impressed with the ridiculous highlighter bouquet.

Chase pulled his cell from his pocket and sent off a quick text to his assistant, putting his next plan into motion. An immediate reply confirmed why Dave was the perfect right-hand man. He would get right on it and now Chase just had to do a little more charming with Miss Shaw. The highlighters were a nice touch, but that gesture had barely scratched the surface of his next tactic.

Chase smiled as he headed toward his in-home gym. He needed to hit the weights, maybe the punching bag, and burn off some energy. He had big plans to carry out and a woman to mentally seduce…though if she wound up in his bed, well, he wouldn't exactly turn her away.

Haley hadn't had time to do much digging on Chase. A whole new flood of résumés came through her inbox, not to mention more flowers she'd had to find room for.

The bouquets were getting ridiculous so she'd started passing them out to coworkers. Now every office in the building had an obscene display and she could at least see her desk again.

Those cupcakes, doughnuts and chocolates had made their way to the break room, too. If she ate everything that had come her way, she'd need a new, bigger wardrobe, and that wasn't something she had time for.

Haley settled back in at her desk and scooted closer to her computer. The bundle of highlighters on her desk caught her attention and she couldn't help but smile. She didn't want to smile at Chase's gift. That's what he wanted her to do. He wanted her to think about him...which was basically all she'd done since their impromptu lunch date.

No, it wasn't a date. It had been a meeting of sorts. She didn't date, never had the time or found a man who interested her enough to pull her from her work.

Yet Chase had done exactly that for one hour. He'd gotten her to leave the office and he'd put very little effort into doing so.

But he'd smiled, he'd been adorable in that overbearing sort of way and he'd offered to donate to Tomorrow's Leaders. Albeit, the donation came at a price. Well, she couldn't be bought. She would just continue to work on other contributions where her social life didn't have to come into play.

Damn that man for making her read too much into him. He wasn't after her, per se. He wanted a position that she could help him with…if she wanted to do such a thing. Which she did not.

Becoming CEO would be up to Josh. Her personal feelings weren't the deciding factor.

"Are you going home any time soon?"

Haley glanced up from her computer screen, which she'd been staring at blankly for the past ten minutes, and spotted Josh.

"In a bit," she told him with a smile.

Josh's dirty-blond hair looked as if he'd been raking his fingers through it over the course of the day. He'd already shed his suit jacket, which he had draped over one arm. He'd loosened his tie and she figured the stress of finding a replacement was getting to him. This was certainly not a decision to be taken lightly.

"I can't believe you're leaving," she added. "It's not even six o'clock yet. You usually have a few more hours in you."

Josh's smile widened. "Sophie made me promise to take off early. She's surprising me with dinner and some other plans she's keeping to herself."

Haley loved that Josh and Sophie had found each other. The two were so in love and Josh had definitely turned into a totally different man because of her. Not so long ago, the stress and CEO position had really been getting to Josh, so much so he would bark orders at her or just be frustrated and act almost as if he didn't want her here.

During those times she cleverly did not point out the fact she'd been here even longer than he had, knew the inner workings as much as he did. When she'd been in college, Haley had actually worked for Vernon Lowell as an intern. Her loyalty to this company was the reason she stayed while almost every other employee bailed when Josh took over. She helped him rebuild Black Crescent.

Recently, Sophie had softened something in Josh, and now Haley almost hated to see him go. He was like the brother she never had. Well, she had a brother, but there was no solid relationship there. Haley was honestly closer with her work family than her actual biological family.

"I hope you have a good night," she told him. "Sounds like fun."

"Speaking of fun, what made you get out for lunch earlier?" he asked, a wry grin on his face as if he knew some dirty little secret.

"Sorry to disappoint." She turned in her chair to face him fully. "It was just a business lunch with an acquaintance."

A really over-the-top-sexy acquaintance who had charmed her into submission.

Not that Haley would tell Josh exactly whom she'd had lunch with, especially since Chase had already had an interview with Josh. Added to that, several weeks ago Sophie had caught Haley and Chase flirting.

Sophie had intervened, asking Haley if everything was okay. Thankfully, Josh knew nothing of this harmless encounter. Haley didn't want to be seen as flirting or dining with a potential prospect for the highest position at Black Crescent. Haley had never slept with a coworker or her boss and she sure as hell didn't intend to start now.

And she hadn't been lying when she'd told Sophie she could handle Chase. She could...until he'd shown up with that absurd gift that ultimately landed her in his car and at his personal table at one of her favorite restaurants.

She'd have to be more vigilant when it came to that sly mogul. She'd also have to get serious about that research so she could uncover more about the man who wanted to become her boss. She needed more hours in the day to get everything done, but this little bit of work couldn't be shared. She didn't want anyone to know her special project on the side. This was totally personal.

"Well, take the night off," Josh told her, pulling her back to the moment. "You've been working too much."

Haley laughed. "Never thought I'd hear you say that. We're both such workaholics."

"I just have a different outlook on life now." Josh shrugged with a wide grin. "I need to get going. Have a good night," he told her before he headed down the hall.

Considering she and Josh were usually the last two to ever leave the building, she had to assume she was alone. Haley pulled up her favorite playlist on her computer and set the music to a higher volume to help distract her from the wayward thoughts regarding a certain billionaire competing for her attention.

As she searched through her emails and hummed along to the songs, Haley was pretty proud of herself for making her way through the bulk of the latest résumés before sending them on to Allison Randall, who would narrow the list even more. Josh wanted only the top three for interviews. With Ryan out, and Chase and Matt already interviewed, that meant they were getting close.

Her cell chimed and she did a quick glance, then stilled. She didn't recognize the number, but with having a charity, she couldn't ignore calls just assuming the other end was a telemarketer.

She paused her music and grabbed her phone. "Hello?"

"Miss Shaw."

That low, familiar voice shouldn't send shivers through her, but here she was trying to tamp them down.

Haley eased back in her seat and pulled in a deep breath. "Mr. Hargrove. I won't insult you by asking how you got my personal number."

His rich laughter slid through the phone and did nothing to help those shivers she was trying to ignore. No man had ever had such an effect on her before. Dates were one thing, kisses were another. Those could lead to shivers… But a voice through the phone? Never.

"I assume you're still at work," he said.

"I am."

"Do you ever leave that office?" he asked.

Haley came to her feet and circled her desk. She crossed to her small refrigerator she kept in the corner and grabbed a bottle of water. She wasn't about to remind him that she did indeed leave the office when she was coerced by a sexy, charming lunch date.

No, not a date. She'd better be more careful where those thoughts wandered. Sexual fantasies were one thing, and something she couldn't avoid, but thinking in terms of dates and an actual relationship could get her into more trouble than she was ready for.

"I take quite a bit of pride in my work," she informed him. "Besides, I'm rather busy trying to fill some very big shoes."

"Yes, the CEO position. What evening do you think you could take some free time for yourself?"

"All to myself?" she countered, taking the bottle back to her desk. "Or are you asking for my time to be spent with you?"

"Beautiful and smart. I like that."

Haley wasn't about to address the *beautiful* comment. Allure oozed off him and words were so easy to string together for someone like Chase. A man with power and money was likely used to getting what he wanted and just assumed all women found him irresistible.

Damn it, she couldn't deny she fell into that category. But what else could she do when sexy was his default mode?

"So what is it exactly that you're trying to ask, Mr. Hargrove?"

She took a seat and crossed her legs, leaning back in her chair and trying to maintain her composure.

"I have Broadway tickets for Wednesday night," he informed her. "I'd like you to join me."

Haley stilled. Broadway tickets? Like…a date? Hadn't she just finished her mental lecture on not dating this guy?

Lunch during business hours was one thing, but

a play with a man trying to become her boss was an entirely different matter.

"I'm not sure that's a good idea."

"I assumed you'd say as much," he retorted with another low chuckle. "What would make you feel better? If we called this a date or if we called this a business meeting?"

She pursed her lips and considered her options. "What would make me feel better is honesty. You called me, so what context did you call me in?"

"A date."

His swift, confident reply had her heart beating faster, her nerves kicking into high gear. Did he really want to ask her out? Could he really be chasing her as a woman and not for the part of her that was a stepping-stone to the most prominent position at Black Crescent?

"And I'm the only woman you could think of to ask?"

"You're the only woman I *wanted* to ask."

Oh, why did he have all the answers, and why was she allowing this fascination to pull her in more and more?

Because she was curious. She couldn't ignore her attraction any more than she could stop the sun from setting. Besides, it was just a play. They couldn't exactly get too carried away in a very public place…right?

"Fine."

"Fine?" he asked, then chuckled. "Well, don't get overly excited about it."

"Mr. Hargrove, if you want someone excited and falling all over herself at the idea of a date with you, then you've asked the wrong woman."

That rich laughter filled the phone and she gripped it tight. Her heart beat even faster and her stomach flopped at the prospect of being out with Chase.

"Oh, I've asked the right woman," he corrected. "And you're going to need to call me Chase since we're dating."

"We're not dating," she corrected.

"Not until Wednesday. I'll see you then, Haley."

He hung up, leaving her speechless and wondering what the hell she'd just agreed to.

Four

"Are you sure this is what you want to do, sir?"

Chase watched through his window as the city streets went by. He paid his driver to drive, not to dole out unsolicited advice. Granted, Al had been Chase's driver for over ten years and he often gave advice…which Chase normally valued.

He didn't want to hear it now. Maybe Chase was making a mistake, but he wanted Haley and that had nothing to do with the revenge or the job and everything to do with the fact that she intrigued him. He couldn't explain why this woman was the one whom he wanted to spend time with, the one he ultimately wanted in his bed.

But he wouldn't ignore what he wanted...not the job and not the woman. There was no reason he couldn't have both.

"I'm positive," Chase replied.

"I'm not sure getting cozy with Haley Shaw is the best move at this time. She's innocent in all of this."

Al knew everything. He knew the backstory of Chase's father going to prison due to the money trail left by Vernon Lowell, and Al was aware that Chase refused to rest until the Lowell family was brought down...even if that meant seeking justice via Vernon's children.

But he was right in the fact that Haley was an innocent. Granted, she'd stuck through the scandal and Vernon's skipping town and then the transition when Josh took over. She had to know everything that went down, but she was ever the loyal employee...and Chase's best option for finding any nugget of inside information he needed to plan his attack.

"She's the in that I have," Chase stated, turning to catch Al's judgmental reflection in the rearview mirror.

There was one secret Al didn't know. There was no way in hell Chase would ever mention that what started out as harmless flirting and using his charms had turned into a full-on attraction that Chase couldn't fight.

He hadn't expected to find her conservative, stuffy exterior so damn sexy. Those slim dresses that hit just past her knee combined with simple nude heels gave him fantasies that he was best to keep to himself.

"I can't talk you out of this, can I?" Al asked as he pulled in front of Haley's house.

Chase smiled. "Just wait here. We'll be back."

Al's sigh of disapproval didn't escape Chase, but he didn't need approval. While he respected Al as much more than a driver, Chase also had to live his own life and make his own decisions... and mistakes.

Taking Haley to a Broadway play wasn't a mistake, though. Bedding her? Well, that might be a mistake, but he wouldn't turn down the opportunity. He certainly hadn't gone into this thinking of seduction, but he also wasn't taking it off the table.

No man in his right mind could ignore the natural, simplistic beauty that Haley offered. The fact that she didn't fall all over herself and almost posed as an unexpected challenge was a hell of a turn-on. Combined with her loyalty to her job... He admired a woman who remained focused.

Still, he had no clue what made her remain so faithful to the Lowell family and Black Crescent. Haley had been with them since college, from everything he'd learned about her. Why the hell would she stay during the scandal when Vernon literally ruined people's lives? How did she justify such actions?

No matter what her reasoning was, that wasn't his problem. He needed to get some scoop from her, anything that would help him in getting ahead and solidifying his revenge.

His cell chimed in his pocket, but he ignored it. Nothing was more important than taking Haley out tonight. Maybe by getting outside the office, after business hours, she would relax and let loose. And perhaps she'd be easier to uncover.

Chase knocked on her door and within minutes Haley stepped out. It took every ounce of Chase's willpower to keep his mouth from dropping.

If he thought she was sexy in those little conventional dresses at the office, that was nothing compared with this sleeveless black jumpsuit with a plunging neckline. She wore a pair of strappy black sandals showing off her red polished toes... He hadn't expected the red.

With her blond hair curled and red glossy lips,

Haley looked completely different from every other time he'd seen her.

And she'd just changed the dynamics of this little game. He didn't know she'd be bringing her arsenal of sex appeal into battle, but he was more than ready to tussle with her. Haley wasn't stupid or naive. She'd dressed like this on purpose with every intention of throwing him off his game.

Well, maybe it would be her who was thrown off. She agreed to this date, so he obviously had some hold over her if she couldn't turn him down. Chase had to make sure he kept the upper hand here or he'd wind up losing sight of everything he'd set out to gain.

Chase composed himself and took a step forward to greet her.

"You look sexy as hell," he murmured when he got closer.

Haley smiled. "It's not often I go on a date, so I wanted to be a little extra tonight."

"I appreciate it."

Haley's eyes leveled his as those red lips curved into a killer smile. "Oh, I did this for me. I love a feeling of empowerment… Don't you?"

She sashayed past him. Chase shook his head as he followed those swaying hips down the front steps.

What in the hell had he gotten himself into? The woman was purposely antagonizing him and clearly loving every second of the torture.

Chase might not know what he'd gotten himself into or how this would ultimately play out, but he knew this task of schmoozing Haley was not going to be boring.

The real question was…just who was seducing whom here?

Haley had no idea how Chase got tickets so last-minute to the most popular show on Broadway, but she didn't care. Their seats were the best, the show was spectacular and now they were walking down the busy city street in Manhattan.

Lights twinkled from each and every building, the warm late-summer air washed over her and people bustled about. She loved this city, especially in the summer. It wasn't often she got away from work to enjoy a social life out on the town. Once the new CEO was in position, she really should take more time for herself and get back into the swing of nightlife and a good time. She was still young, she still had memories to make.

"You up for a drink?" he asked.

"I have to be at work early in the morning," she told him.

He slid his hand into hers as if that were the most normal next step into this evening. Everything about this night felt like a real date. He hadn't brought up work, which was both surprising and refreshing.

"One drink," he promised. "I know the perfect place."

No doubt he knew the perfect place, a place where he took all his ladies. She didn't want to fall in that same line of the women he had a pattern with. She wasn't one of his usual dates and she didn't want to think of this as anything more than what it was…a game.

While she wasn't quite sure his angle or why he was going to such lengths to charm her, she had to keep her guard up. Having a bit of fun in the process wouldn't hurt anything. A little flirting, sexual banter, maybe even a fling… But anything that happened would be on her terms and because she wanted it to progress. Chase couldn't, and wouldn't, have a hold over her.

Yeah, right. Just keep telling yourself that.

"One drink," she replied. "But only because I'm out of Pinot at home."

And there went that rich laughter again. That pure male, all rough-and-low laughter she'd come to associate with him. The weeks of flirting and harmless banter had somehow led them to this night, and she wasn't sorry she'd said yes. Quite the opposite. Haley was well aware of what this was and what it wasn't.

Chase wasn't out for some exclusivity or a relationship. He wasn't out for even a fling. He wanted to get that top slot and he was really going all out to win her affection.

"I'll have to make a note to get you a box of Pinot," he told her. "I know a wonderful distributor. They can be at your door first thing in the morning."

Haley glanced his way as he assisted her toward the next block. "I think that's a bit of overkill, don't you? I mean, what would I do with an entire box?"

"Throw a dinner party," he suggested. "Or maybe go smaller and invite someone over to help you drink it. Glasses optional. I think other, more intimate ways could be the theme."

He threw her a glance that had her head spinning and visions forming. Late nights with a glass of wine on the balcony off her bedroom before moving into her oversize master and having the pale liquor poured all over her while Chase's tongue traveled the same path—

"How many students are you going to fund this fall?"

His question caught her off guard and had her mind spinning in another direction. "Excuse me?"

"With your charity," he added, guiding her across another busy intersection as if he hadn't just put a naughty thought in her head. "How many teens were you able to fund?"

"Oh, um, eighteen. I'm hoping we can squeeze a couple more out of the applicants that came through."

"Do you get much else done besides looking at résumés and applications?" he asked. "Between the charity and Black Crescent, I mean."

Haley hadn't thought about her work in that manner, but she actually didn't get much else done.

With a shrug, she smiled. "I love what I do. Both jobs. I wouldn't have it any other way."

"You're clearly giving your time to everyone around you. Is that why you don't date much?"

He gestured toward a doorway with a large black-and-gold awning. Thankfully, they were here and she didn't have to dive into the boring whys of her social life. Couldn't someone just enjoy her work? Why did she have to defend her lifestyle to someone who didn't even know her?

In no time, she and Chase were escorted up the stairs and into a private room with their own bartender. But of course they were. Why would he take a seat at the bar with common folk when money talked and he could have privacy?

Haley took a seat at an intimate, curved booth. Chase slid in beside her, but he didn't crowd her. They placed their drink orders and were left alone. Haley couldn't ignore the tingle of arousal that coursed through her. The way Chase had looked at her all night, the simple way he took her hand— she might be a helpless romantic, but those were the little things that got to her.

The sexy man in the suit didn't hurt, either. There was something to be said about a well-dressed man who knew how to fill out a tailor-made jacket.

"We could have sat down in the bar," she told him.

Chase flashed her a smile and eased his arm along the back of the bench. "We could have, but then I wouldn't be able to hear you. If you want good music, though, downstairs is the place to be. I happen to know the owner."

"Are you the owner?" she asked.

Chase laughed. "No, but we went to college together."

"Harvard? Yale? I can't remember what Ivy League school you indicated on your résumé."

He shook his head and leveled that dark stare

her way. "Hardly Ivy League. I went to Ithaca on a football scholarship and I studied business. I was smart in school, but nothing an Ivy League school would've looked twice at. My family couldn't have afforded for me to go anywhere without my scholarship, so I'm just thankful I was athletic."

Interesting. That was a whole side of him she didn't know. A man who came from meager beginnings to make a name for himself and become a billionaire mogul was quite impressive. Maybe he wasn't the egotistical man she'd first believed. There was nothing wrong with an ego, but now that she knew he warranted that sense of pride, she could appreciate him so much more.

The bartender delivered their drinks and promptly left them. Haley took a sip of her Pinot and toyed with the stem of her crystal glass.

"I went to community college," she found herself saying before she could stop herself. "I have zero athletic ability. My only hobbies are singing off-key in the shower or making spreadsheets in my sleep."

Chase's chuckle seemed so genuine, not like he was purposely trying to appease her or keep her attention solely on him.

"I'm sure you have talents," he stated. "You don't have to be athletic."

"I played softball once." She lifted her glass and took another sip. "It was a short-lived career. I was eight and I did cartwheels around the bases instead of running them during warm-ups."

Chase's lips twitched as if he was holding back his laugh. "And did you end up taking gymnastics?"

"No. My parents couldn't afford lessons." She glanced to her glass and slid her thumb up the delicate stem. "I didn't always see eye to eye with them about most things anyway."

"Are you close now?"

Haley shook her head. "We still don't have the same vision."

"They have to be proud of your work," he replied, shifting to face her better. "You've become quite successful."

Haley smiled and pulled in a breath. "To them, I'm a secretary. Nothing near as exciting as a doctor or lawyer like they wanted my brother to be."

"And is your brother a doctor or lawyer?"

Haley shook her head again. "No. They paid for him to go to a fancy college and he ended up flunking out. Too much partying, but that's none of my business."

"How can they not be proud of all the work

you've done?" he asked. "You've been with Black Crescent for so long, you're irreplaceable."

Haley bit the inside of her cheek to keep from laughing. She always felt like she was invaluable, too, but that was just her battered ego. She liked to think that they couldn't live without her, but if she left, someone would replace her and the company would keep running.

"You really do know how to get on someone's good side," she informed him. "Flattery doesn't always get you to the top."

"No, but my impeccable résumé will." He flashed that killer grin once again and took a sip of his bourbon. "Everyone knows you're the backbone of that operation. Who knows what would've happened all those years ago during that scandal if you hadn't stayed on."

"I was just an intern back then."

"Who was far more knowledgeable than most," he retorted. "When Josh stepped into the role of CEO, I guarantee you were the one who had to get him going and made him look good to the general public."

Haley shrugged. She didn't need accolades or credit for her work. She truly enjoyed helping others, and just because Josh's father had been a liar and a cheat didn't mean Josh or his brothers were the same.

Many people in the town didn't feel that way, though. Some still blamed Josh for Vernon's actions. The brothers had all been held under a microscope when their father split, but Josh was the one who had truly stuck, trying to salvage the family name and business.

"So what's your angle here?" she asked Chase, smiling when he quirked a brow. "You want the CEO position so bad that you're willing to fake date me? Or is there something else you're after?"

His eyes darkened as they dropped to her lips. She realized her open-ended question held too many possible answers the moment the words had slipped out.

"Oh, there are several things I want, Haley."

You can bet they center on that promised shipment of wine.

She'd put herself in this position. She'd wanted to know what it would be like to go out with someone like Chase, knowing she had the upper hand because he needed her.

But now? Well, she wasn't so sure her control hadn't slipped. If she wasn't careful, she'd wind up in bed with the man, and just her luck, he'd also become her boss.

Haley leaned in closer and murmured, "Sex isn't on the table."

"No?"

He kept that dark gaze on her. Part of her wanted to back away, come to the realization that Chase wasn't in all this for her. But the other part wanted to ignore those waving red flags and see what would happen if she just leaned in a little. Would he close that distance between them and put his lips where his eyes had been? Would she let him?

Yes, she would. She wanted to know what those lips would feel like. She wanted to feel his hands glide over her bare body. Would that fantasy ever become reality?

"I'm aware I'm not actually your type," she informed him, picking up her glass and draining it. "But I'm going to figure out your angle. I can't believe you're going through all of this just to land a position at Black Crescent."

He eased over in the bench, his arm sliding even farther behind her back as he leaned in closer to her face. Those eyes once again dropped to her lips and she couldn't stop that knee-jerk reaction of licking them.

Anticipation soared through her. Was this when he'd kiss her? Was this when she'd welcome that much-awaited touch?

"Maybe I'm trying to land you," he murmured against her lips.

Haley couldn't suppress the shivers and couldn't deny the flirting and fun and games had taken a new direction, and she wasn't sure which way she was supposed to go.

Five

"Are you with me?"

Haley blinked away the daydream and stared up at her boss. Josh stood in front of her desk, one hand in his pocket, the other holding a résumé.

"I'm sorry. What?"

His brows drew in. "Is everything okay? You seem off this morning."

Maybe that's because she was left hanging for that kiss last night on her date/nondate with Chase. Maybe because the man was driving her out of her ever-loving mind as she tried to anticipate his next move. Or maybe she should remove herself from this crazy ride she'd gotten on and save her own sanity.

"Yes, I'm fine," she assured him with a smile.

Haley came to her feet and straightened her pencil dress. "You were saying?"

Josh stared at her another minute before glancing down to the paper in his hand. "I was saying that I'd like to set up a second interview with Matt Velez. Remember I told you I talked to him outside of the office? I'd like to bring him in again."

Haley was well aware of Matt's résumé. Along with Allison, they'd vetted each and every one that had come through. Haley wasn't sure Matt was the perfect applicant for the job of CEO, but she was also slowly getting swayed by her hormones and not her common sense.

She had an obligation to the company to help secure a solid future, which also meant her job and many others. She couldn't let Chase and his methodical plans to woo her hinder her decisions.

"I'll get that interview set up right away," she assured Josh. "Do you prefer Monday morning after your conference call?"

"That's fine. I know it's short notice, but see if Allison can fly in for it. And like the other ones, I want you in there with me," he told her. "It's only fair that you have a say over who you'll be working closely with. After all, you're the one who will be with our new CEO the most."

Haley nodded, pleased that he was taking her feelings into consideration. But if she had to weigh in on whom she wanted to spend most of her days and evenings with here at the office, her answer certainly wasn't Matt.

A commanding man with dark brown eyes and light brown messy hair came into mind. The man with broad shoulders, perfectly tailored suits and heavy-lidded eyes who made her think only of rustled sheets and sleepless nights.

"Haley?"

"I'll get it scheduled," she told him, forcing herself back to the moment and her duties. "No problem."

"Is there anything you want to tell me?" he asked, brows drawn in.

Josh cared about each of his employees. Haley had come to think of him as a friend, someone she could trust and rely on. But there was no way she could confess what was truly going on. He wouldn't understand and he likely wouldn't like that she'd been technically dating one of the applicants.

Haley reached for the résumé and laid the paper on her desk. "I'm just a little distracted, but nothing that will affect my job."

Well, that was somewhat of a lie considering she spent a good portion of her time fantasizing when she should be focusing on the next phase of Black Crescent.

Josh sighed and slid his hands into his pockets. "You know you can talk to me," he told her.

"Just a date I had the other night," she confessed. "I'm trying to tell myself he's not the guy for me, but it's getting more difficult because I'm developing feelings I really shouldn't have."

Josh's intense stare quickly turned amused as a wide grin spread across his face. "I didn't think Sophie was for me, either, but look how that turned out. I didn't realize you were dating anyone."

Neither did she, and she wasn't quite sure what to call all of this she and Chase were doing. He was toying with her. He had to be. But she was human with very real feelings and she couldn't stop her attraction. She had to believe he was attracted; either that or he was a damn good actor.

Still, that didn't mean she could let her guard down. Chase wasn't gullible and he wasn't stupid. He was meticulous and no doubt had a well-laid plan. She just had to make sure she stayed one step ahead of him.

"Well, we only had one date," she explained to Josh. "I've just been so wrapped up in work and Tomorrow's Leaders, I haven't had much of a social life lately. I'm sure I'm making a big deal out of nothing."

"Don't discount your feelings," he warned. "You're allowed to have a social life and you're also allowed to leave before it gets dark outside, you know."

Haley laughed. "I'm aware, but I feel guilty when there's so much to be done to get ready for the transition of the CEO."

"You stood by this company when the shit hit the fan with my dad. I have no doubt whatsoever that you will make the next transition smooth, and anyone who takes my place will be thankful to have you."

She wasn't one who thrived on compliments; that's not why she did her job. But she wasn't going to ignore Josh's praise by blowing off his kind words.

"I appreciate that," she told him. "I'll get this interview set up for Monday."

"Great." He started to turn away but stopped and met her gaze once again. "Whoever this guy is, he's damn lucky to have you."

Haley smiled and simply nodded her silent appreciation.

How did she explain that she went on a date with an applicant? Or the fact that, while there was most definitely sexual tension, she wasn't fully convinced that he had the truest of intentions.

The next morning, Haley took a seat at her desk and opened a new tab on her computer. She didn't necessarily have the time to devote to extra work right now, but she needed to dig deeper into Chase Hargrove.

Instead of fantasizing about him, she had to find out who he really was. Haley wanted to know more behind the man, more about his motives for seeking out not only the CEO position, but also for being so aggressive in pursuing her.

She went to one site, then another, falling down the rabbit hole of this world-renowned investment mogul. He had a home in Cannes for which he'd paid over twenty million dollars, and Haley found herself basking in the view for just a moment before moving on.

She couldn't even imagine owning a home like that or even having the time to get away for a luxury vacation. Clearly Chase had made some damn good investments and took care of his clients or he wouldn't be able to afford such extravagance.

And knowing a sliver of his background and that he came from meager beginnings made this revelation all the more impressive.

The further back she went into his world, the

more she realized he was much more than what was on his résumé.

He also hadn't been born Chase Hargrove. When the hell had he changed his name, and why? There had to be a story there because from what she could tell, his parents were still married, so the name change didn't make much sense.

Maybe digging into his parents was the way to go. Were they all estranged? He hadn't mentioned any such thing during their dinner the other night.

Yet more secrets she wanted to uncover.

When her cell chimed on her desk, Haley jumped. She glanced to see Chase's name lighting up the screen. She thought about letting him go to voice mail, but she couldn't deny the man and she wondered if that would ultimately be her downfall.

She liked to tell herself she wasn't saying no to him simply because she wanted to learn more... But in reality she wasn't saying no because she was selfish and wanted more. She just wished she knew where her curiosity would end up taking her and how far she'd let this game play out.

Pushing away from her computer, Haley turned to grab her phone.

"Good morning," she answered.

Chase's familiar chuckle slid through the line. "Nope, it's now noon."

She glanced to her computer screen and he was right. Obviously she'd fallen down the rabbit hole of Chase's life. Not that she would ever admit any such thing to him.

"You caught me," she replied. "It's been quite the morning."

Like finding out he wasn't exactly who he said he was. She wondered why, but that was something she'd definitely be finding out. If she flat out asked him, would he tell her the truth?

"Are you free tonight?" he asked.

"Depends on what you had in mind."

Another date? Did she want to keep getting tangled with a man who obviously had ulterior motives?

Yes, she did. She was intrigued, she was charmed... She was turned on. She simply couldn't turn off such strong emotions. Chase was a powerful man in more ways than one.

"I'll take that to mean you're free."

His low, gravelly voice did crazy things to her hormones. Things she hadn't felt in far too long, which made them impossible to ignore.

Why couldn't she get a grip with this guy? Why couldn't she just deny him and move on?

Because he'd left her wondering what those lips would feel like against hers. He'd left her wondering if he wanted her just as much as she wanted him. There was really only one way to find out.

"I can pick you up at your place at six if you're up for a surprise," he added.

She leaned back in her seat and stared at her screen, seeing the evidence in black-and-white that he wasn't on the up-and-up. But she never backed down from a challenge—hence why she was still at Black Crescent even after all of the scandal and their tarnished reputation. She'd stuck by Josh's side during the most difficult time when it would have been all too easy to pack up and leave like everyone else did.

So, Haley wasn't about to shy away from Chase. Didn't everyone have a few skeletons in their closet?

"I'll be ready," she told him. "But can I ask what I should be ready for? Are we skydiving or watching a movie? I need to dress accordingly."

Once again he laughed, and she hated how such a simple act could produce so many emotions. The arousal, the excitement, the thrill of the chase—though she still wasn't sure who was chasing whom.

"And what would you wear for skydiving?" he asked.

"Probably a blindfold because I'd be terrified," she joked.

"Bring that blindfold," he stated. "I'm sure we can find a better use for it."

The instant erotic image filled her mind and she knew without a doubt that he was crossing the line of flirting, and she didn't mind one bit. She was human, she was a woman with basic needs. Why should she deny having a little harmless fun?

Oh, right. Because he could end up being her boss at one point and she knew he was lying about something.

All of that still didn't squash her desires or turn off her attraction. The blindfold comment left her more than intrigued about what might or might not turn him on. She wouldn't mind digging into his fetishes.

"I'll be ready at six," she informed him. "Sans blindfold."

"Fine by me. I have a few you can borrow. See you then."

He hung up, leaving her wondering if he was serious or joking about that blindfold collection. Every part of her had a feeling he was quite serious, and that only aroused her even more.

How had they gone from harmless flirting to discussing veiled sexual games? Chase was a smooth one since she didn't have a clue how to answer that question. It was those smooth ones who could get a girl into trouble…but oh, the best kind.

Haley sighed and put her phone back on her desk, turning her focus back to the computer and back to the hunt to find the real Chase. She wondered why he changed his last name. What made him want to take on another? Surely he didn't have a falling-out with his parents. Or maybe he did. That was certainly something she could easily find.

She didn't have too much time to keep devoting to Chase today, but she wasn't done digging. Perhaps on their date he might divulge a little more and she could slowly uncover what type of man he truly was...other than sexy as hell and too charming for his own good.

He never did tell her exactly what they were doing or how she should dress. Still, surprises were fun. She didn't remember the last time someone surprised her with anything...save for the slew of flowers and pastries that came through from would-be applicants.

Pushing aside thoughts of Chase and any other distractions, Haley turned her attention to the latest résumés Allison had vetted. There was still a position to be filled and Haley wanted the absolute best possible candidate, considering she truly loved this company and she'd have to be working with that said individual day in and day out.

Part of her couldn't help but imagine Chase in

that role. What would he be like as a boss? Could they even have a standard working relationship?

Granted, they hadn't actually crossed any lines physically, but mentally… Hell, she'd crossed them all several times. If they ended up in bed, how could they turn back and go to boss/assistant?

An instant image of him sweeping off his desk and laying her down filled her mind. She couldn't just ignore the need she had or the possibilities that rolled through her.

Chase Hargrove, or whatever his last name used to be, wasn't in the CEO position just yet, so that still made him free game. If he was going to come on to her like he wanted her, Haley was going to show him just how much she wanted him. There was no code of ethics that said she couldn't have a social life with an applicant.

If he was playing some sort of game with her, then she'd make him regret it. But what if there was no game? What if he actually wanted her and wanted to be CEO of Black Crescent Hedge Fund? There was no reason he couldn't want both, right?

And if that was the case, she had a feeling Chase Hargrove might just become a permanent fixture in her life…in one way or another.

Six

Haley sank deeper into the corner of her sectional sofa and curled her feet beneath her. Like most companies with summer hours, Black Crescent had short Fridays. After Chase's call, she finished a few things then packed up and headed home for the afternoon.

With the much-needed extra time, she planned to work on finalizing submissions for Tomorrow's Leaders, but she had already finished going through the list and she still had a few hours before Chase was due to pick her up for her date.

And she'd spent her time wisely, considering she uncovered more about him than she ever thought possible.

Haley stared at the computer screen, utterly stunned at the evidence she'd found. Her questions about Chase's motives were answered, but she didn't like what she'd uncovered and was almost sorry she'd been digging.

Chase's father, Dale Groveman, had done business years ago with Vernon Lowell. When everything with Vernon and Black Crescent exploded, apparently Dale took some of the fall and landed in prison.

According to everything Haley had found, that was about the time Chase's mother moved into a low-income apartment from their ritzy home out in the country. Then she was hospitalized shortly after at a mental health facility, but those records were sealed tight. Haley could only imagine the poor woman had a nervous breakdown considering there had been no prior medical issues.

They had lost everything and no doubt Chase was out for revenge. Her heart hurt for his family and so many others who had been affected by Vernon's actions. But was Chase using her? Was he interested in her on a personal level or only interested in using her as leverage in his plan to possibly destroy the company she'd loved for so long?

Haley closed her laptop, not wanting to see any more. She'd learned enough to have her mind shooting in all directions. There was a yawning ache deep in the pit of her stomach, one that she feared wouldn't be fixed anytime soon. She'd allowed herself to get swept up in this web. While she wanted to curse herself for being naive, she also had that sliver of hope that Chase wasn't only taking advantage of her. He seemed genuinely interested… Didn't he? Was he that focused on revenge that he'd turned into a hell of a good actor?

Had Chase targeted her specifically because he thought she would be easy access to get into Black Crescent? Did he like her as a woman at all or was everything an act?

Too many questions to try to decipher answers on her own. Only time would tell because she couldn't exactly go to him and flat out ask. She needed to play this smart and be cautious.

While the hurt continued to slide deep into her, this was nothing new to Haley. People had underestimated her for as long as she could remember. Her parents didn't think she was good enough or smart enough like her brother, which was why they'd invested all of their money into his schooling and not hers.

When she'd started as an intern at Black Crescent Hedge Fund, she'd been seen only as a young blonde with a curvy figure, so what could she possibly know?

Well, look at her now. She'd been around the longest and was the right-hand woman to the CEO. She was damn proud of herself for all she'd accomplished. True, she could go somewhere else with her credentials, but she loved this company and they had always given her the time she needed to work on her own charity.

Her mind circled back to Chase. She still didn't know why he'd changed his last name or what his plans were exactly, but she wasn't about to just let him do anything he wanted or try to harm this company in any way.

Turning the tables wouldn't be easy, but she was up for the challenge. First thing would be to get ready for this date and use every weapon in her arsenal. A killer outfit, sexy heels... She didn't mind making him suffer a little because she would maintain control of this situation now that she had a better handle on his motives.

If only she knew his exact plan...

Haley sat her computer on the coffee table and headed toward her en suite. A relaxing bubble bath would help calm her because she had a feeling she was getting ready to dive into a hell of a storm.

* * *

"That was the most amazing thing ever."

Haley's excitement seemed to radiate off her. Her smile widened, her eyes lit up and she seemed completely relaxed…just how he wanted her.

Of course, he was anything but relaxed since he'd picked her up and she'd come out wearing another sexy-as-hell jumpsuit. This one had a halter top, leaving her back exposed and taunting him with all that pale, creamy skin. The pants had slits that went high up onto her thigh, and the material had separated when she'd sat in the seat next to him in the theater. It had been all he could do not to toy with that high V over her leg and see just how far she was willing to let him go.

He'd started this charade months ago with harmless flirting, but he'd had no idea just how much being with Haley Shaw would affect him as a man.

When he'd first set out to destroy the Lowells, he honestly had no idea he'd come in contact with anyone as intriguing, as sexy or as challenging as Haley. Under other circumstances, he'd date her, seduce her the proper way and not have these damn guilty feelings getting in the way of his goals.

Damn it. He wanted Haley and it had nothing to do with the job or his revenge plot. She intrigued him, she aroused him and she flat out got under his skin in ways he'd never allowed another woman.

Chase slid his hand into hers as he led her back to his car. He'd given Al the night off, as he wanted total privacy with Haley.

"All I did was take you to see a movie," he told her.

She jerked her attention to his. "That wasn't just any movie," she reminded him. "That was an early premiere of the biggest blockbuster that will hit cinemas this year. I don't know how you managed the private showing, but that movie had been on my list since all the hype around it last year."

"I'm glad you enjoyed it. The producer is actually a friend of mine, so I had a strong connection."

As they reached his car, Chase maneuvered her toward it, expertly spinning her until her back was pressed against the door. He leaned in, one hand on either side of her shoulders.

Haley's eyes widened, then dropped to his mouth. Arousal slammed into him, but he kept control over his emotions.

"Are you going to kiss me now?" she asked, her lips quirking into a slight grin as if she were daring him.

"It's time, don't you think?"

"Past time."

Chase leaned in closer, surprised and utterly

turned on even more when her hands came up to frame his face as she pulled him down to meet her lips. She opened for him, threading her fingers through his hair, taking the kiss like she'd been starving for his touch.

He understood that all-consuming need. Since seeing her in her office on day one in her conservative dress up until now with her inner vixen coming out for their date, Chase was hanging on by a very thin thread.

Damn the job and his revenge. He wanted Haley with a fierceness that he'd never known. Why her? Why now? He was supposed to be focused on the plan he'd set into motion years ago. He'd waited for the perfect opening into Black Crescent and here it was…only this sexy distraction stood in his way and he had no clue where she fit in. Oh, wait. She didn't. There was no plan for a hot fling with the sexy assistant.

Chase trailed his fingertips over her bare arms, eliciting a shiver from her that racked into his own body. He'd thought he could control this kiss, but he wasn't so sure now.

How did one woman have so much power over him? How could she make him forget his goals, his well-thought-out plans of revenge and redemption?

Because she was sexy as hell, she was loyal to a

fault—a trait he could understand and appreciate—
and she challenged him in ways no woman ever had.

Haley laced her fingers through his hair and
shifted, aligning their bodies in a way that left no
doubt how turned on he was.

Chase reached down to her hips, gripping them
in his hands, and held her still. He wanted her,
but out here in a parking lot was certainly not the
place. He'd planned on only a quick kiss, something to take the sexual edge off, but all he'd done
was fan the proverbial flames.

Chase forced himself to ease away. Haley's lids
slowly opened as she focused her attention on him.

"That was intense," she murmured. "And long
overdue."

Chase agreed on both counts, but wasn't about
to say anything. He needed to maintain his head
about him, to focus, but Haley was charming, more
so than he'd originally noticed. She had a heart
of gold with her charity—one he'd looked up and
thoroughly investigated.

He didn't want her getting caught up in the middle of his anger and retaliation. Chase wanted to
go after Vernon himself, but since the old bastard
was still MIA fifteen years later, Josh Lowell was
next in line. There were other sons, but Josh was
the one who had taken over Daddy's reins.

"Are you ready for the next phase of the date?" he asked.

Haley's brows rose. "Was that kiss a stepping-stone?"

Chase laughed, unable to ignore the way her brazen, bold attitude turned him on even more. At any other point in his life, he would love to see just where this fiery spirit led him, but he had to stay on track.

"Actually, we have reservations and we're going to be late if we don't get moving."

Haley slid her hands to his shoulders. "And would being late be such a bad thing?"

Honestly? He was ready to forget dinner and these reservations altogether. There was nothing he wanted more than to yank the silky tie around her neck and see that black material float down over her breasts. He wanted her alone, with no distractions, no outside forces giving him reasons they shouldn't be intimate.

If they'd met under different circumstances, he would've already had her in his bed. But he'd deceived her from the start and because he'd respected her as a woman, he'd taken this slower than he'd ever taken a seduction.

There was going to come a breaking point, though, and he had a feeling that moment would be sooner rather than later.

"Being late wouldn't be a bad thing," he finally replied. "But when I have you, it won't be quick and it won't be from making out in a parking lot."

He didn't miss the way her eyes widened at the term *when*. That's right. There was no more second-guessing where this was going because they both wanted it, and he wasn't going to ignore that sexual pull or deny either of them any longer.

"Awfully sure of yourself," she told him with a slight grin.

"Or maybe I'm sure of you," he countered as he slid his lips over hers before releasing her. "You're the type of woman who goes after what she wants. Am I right?"

Her eyes grazed over him, an emotion he couldn't quite identify coming over her.

"You have no idea how right you are," she replied.

As he helped her into the car, Chase couldn't help but wonder where he'd started to lose control. But if he didn't regain a hold over this situation, he was going to find himself lost and swept into Haley's world...where he had absolutely no business going.

Seven

"This view is ridiculously breathtaking."

Haley stared out at the skyline of Manhattan from their corner table on the third floor of The Pavilion. The setting sun cast a breathtaking orange and dark pink glow across the horizon. There was something so intimate about sharing a cozy dinner in a posh restaurant while the day came to an end.

Haley had been here only one other time for the wedding of a college friend, but that had been it and she'd always wanted to dine here with a romantic date.

She wasn't sure this fell into the romantic category, but her date fantasies were most definitely fulfilled—sexy man, sunset, dinner and wine.

"I couldn't agree more."

Haley turned her attention back to Chase and noted he wasn't looking at the skyline at all, but directly at her with a hunger in his eyes she recognized all too well.

She shouldn't fall for those perfect one-liners, but she couldn't help herself. He was damn good at this game. The kiss had left her wanting so much more, even though she knew she shouldn't.

Haley had no idea where he was going with his plans. She knew his motivation, but she had to keep on her toes or someone would end up getting hurt.

She pulled in a deep breath and leaned forward, resting her arms on the table. She had to know more about his motives, about the man who was even more mysterious than she'd first thought.

"Tell me why you want to be CEO of Black Crescent Hedge Fund."

To his credit, he didn't look surprised, but he did give a crooked smile and leveled her gaze. That lethal combo was what had landed her here to begin with. She couldn't turn down his charming words and his devilish looks.

So she was human. So what? She didn't know

another woman who would turn down the advances of Chase Hargrove.

"Are we starting the second round of interviews already?" he asked.

Haley shrugged. "I'm just your date trying to get to know you better."

He kept his stare on hers as he leaned back in his seat. "Over the years, I've traveled and started up many investment companies. I know what it takes to make a successful company run smoothly, and Black Crescent is in my hometown. I love the people here and want to ultimately settle down."

Settle down? She hadn't expected that part. A man like Chase Hargrove seemed more the jet-setting, panty-dropping type than the wife, kids and minivan guy.

"So you're sliding into a family-man role, as well?"

He lifted a shoulder and grinned. "Someday. Family is very important to me and nobody would be happier about this than my mother, who reminds me often that she has no grandchildren."

So they weren't estranged. That helped her put another piece of the puzzle together. And he'd just handed her the perfect segue into her line of questioning, though her thoughts tumbled over one another because she had an instant visual of Chase in the role of a father and he just became even sexier.

"So, no siblings?" she asked, reaching for her glass of wine. "Were you terribly spoiled?"

She tried to remain calm, but her insides were a bundle of nerves. Between the growing attraction and tension and all of the unknowns surrounding Chase and his plot, Haley wasn't sure which emotion would overtake her first. This was all new territory for her, but she had to remain loyal to Black Crescent and Josh. They were like her family and she wanted to keep them protected at all costs—even if that meant sacrificing her own happiness.

But when Chase had kissed her, she'd gotten lost. Having his lips and hands on her had made her forget that she even needed to uncover his truths to begin with.

"Not much," he explained. "My mother had a large family, but she was unable to have any more children after me, and I definitely pulled my weight around the house. Maybe that's why I want a family. I want a houseful of children and a wife."

"Someday," she reminded him with a smile.

"Exactly. I'm in no rush."

And it was silly of her to instantly have thoughts pop into her head of being that said wife. She wasn't ready for marriage. She barely had time to do her laundry, let alone feed into a committed, long-term relationship. And children? She really loved her career, so she hadn't thought much about having a family.

Considering her background, she wouldn't even know what to do with a family of her own. Could she even be affectionate? Could she be supportive and loving? As much as she'd like to say yes, she honestly didn't know. There wasn't much to fall back on by way of role models in her past.

"So are you close to your parents?" she asked, toying with the stem of her wineglass.

Dinner had been served and removed long ago, yet they still remained chatting and drinking. Haley was in no hurry to see this night end. She rather enjoyed the company of a sexy, mysterious man.

"Very close," he replied. "My mother was ill for a while years ago and my father wasn't able to care for her during that time. It was a difficult period for all of us, but I think we are stronger as a unit now than ever before."

Obviously that was the time she'd uncovered when they'd moved into a smaller place and his father went to prison. But she still wasn't 100 percent sure how his mother had been sick, though Haley had her suspicions.

"Is your mother okay now?" Haley asked, sincerely wanting to know.

Chase blew out a sigh and sat forward. "She's

amazing. We all bounced back. Not much can keep us down."

"Determination is a big component of running a company," she told him.

He smiled and reached across the table to slide his hand over hers. "Determination is all I have these days."

The way he locked his eyes on hers and delivered such a statement with such conviction, Haley didn't know if they were talking business or not anymore.

"Care to carry this conversation back to my place?" he asked.

Those bold eyes continued to captivate her and she found herself nodding before she could fully think of why this was not a good idea.

"Why should I do that?" she asked. "You could end up being my boss if you have your way about this."

He leaned farther across the table, lifting her hand slightly and lacing his fingers with hers.

"I saw the sunset with you and now I want to see the sunrise."

Her heart tumbled and something clicked into place...something she hadn't known was missing. It wasn't just the sultry words; it was the fact she wanted this man. She wanted him from the moment he'd stopped into the office the very first time. She wanted him when he'd flirted with her over a bundle of silly highlighters. And she wanted him because she recognized determination and that was one very strong common thread they shared.

Maybe they wanted totally different things out of life and maybe he was trying to take down the company she loved so much. But this was just one night. Sex had nothing to do with the job and she was entitled to a social life, right?

For once she was putting her career aside for a night. Tomorrow, she would go back to being on the hunt for the secrets and motives Chase kept hidden. Who knows, maybe she would uncover something at his house. Maybe he'd slip and tell her a nugget of information that she could use to solve this mystery.

Haley wasn't giving up on finding out what he had planned, but she also wasn't giving up on this attraction. The sexual pull was too strong, too overwhelming.

She squeezed his hand and smiled. "I'd love to see that sunrise with you."

Chase hadn't planned on inviting Haley back to his place, but seeing her in that cast of the sunset, looking like she'd never seen anything more beautiful, had really given him a punch of lust to the gut.

Knowing she'd come from such a humble background and knowing how determined and loyal she was only made her that much more attractive. As crazy as it sounded, she was turning into someone he wanted to spend time with, someone he wanted to *be* with, and his newfound emotions had nothing to do with Black Crescent.

He knew he wanted her. That had never been a secret. But he also didn't want her hurt in the end. Nothing would make him give up his revenge against the Lowells. Absolutely nothing.

All he could do at this point in the game was make sure Haley was out of the direct line of fire. When he ultimately took down the company, he would make sure she had a very well-paid, well-positioned place within one of his own companies. He respected her, trusted her, and he couldn't blame her for anything that took place regarding the scandal that Vernon Lowell had orchestrated.

Chase pulled into the drive of his three-story home on the cliffs overlooking the river. He pushed aside all thoughts of Vernon. The old rogue man had been in the forefront of his mind and the main component of this revenge plot for years, but tonight, the only person Chase wanted occupying his mind, and his bed, was the beauty beside him.

Finally, he'd be able to peel her out of her clothes, just like he'd wanted to since he first saw her. He loved how she was conservative by day, but a little sultry, a little more of a vixen, at night.

The perfect woman…if he was looking for such a thing.

Chase pulled into the garage and closed the door behind him. He killed the engine, then turned to face Haley. Only the glow from the overhead garage light illuminated the car, but that was more than enough to see the desire in her eyes and the way her tongue darted out to moisten her bottom lip.

"You're sure about this?" he asked, not wanting to force her into anything she wasn't ready for.

Without a word, Haley leaned over the console and curled her hand around the back of his neck, pulling him toward her as she covered his mouth with hers.

Within the confined space, Chase didn't have the room to touch her like he wanted, like he'd been craving for weeks. He did maneuver one hand up to stroke the side of her face, then he trailed his fingertips down the column of her throat and into the deep V of her halter top.

She trembled beneath his touch and his arousal slammed into him. He wanted out of this car to where he had the freedom to do what he wanted to the woman he craved more than anything else.

At this moment, he craved her more than any revenge…and that was a hell of a dangerous game to play with himself.

Chase eased back and smoothed her hair from her face. Her warm breath washed over him. Her taste on his lips only urged him to hurry this process into the house.

He exited the car and went around to help her out, but by the time he circled the vehicle, she was out, staring at him like he was her every walking fantasy. The feeling was quite mutual, especially with her lips swollen from his. He couldn't wait to explore her passion further, to see her come undone at his touch.

Haley slid her hand into his and he led her into the house. The dim lights turned on as he made his way through to the sunken living area with an entire wall of windows. The sun had all but set and the twinkling lights across the river reflected off the blackened water.

"Your home is gorgeous," she stated, sounding almost surprised and impressed.

Chase didn't know why her approval made his chest puff with pride. Perhaps because his family had lost everything, including their pride, at the hands of the company Haley was so damn loyal to.

Refusing to ever be vulnerable like his parents, Chase clawed his way to the top. When his father had gone to prison and his mother had a nervous breakdown, their bank accounts had been wiped out and their home had been repossessed. Chase had vowed in that dire moment to never, ever be dependent on anyone ever again. He vowed to never let anyone have that much control over his life because everything could be taken away in a single second.

"This view is what sold me on the place," he told her as he gestured toward the impressive set of windows.

Haley stepped down into the living room and crossed to the glass wall. The reflection gave him the opportunity to see her both from the front and the back, offering him the best view of this remarkably sexy woman.

She stood there a moment, taking in the sights before she glanced over her shoulder.

"Do you bring many women here to seduce them?"

Chase couldn't help but smile at her bold question. "I'm not so sure I'm the one doing the seducing here."

Her brow quirked as her eyes gave him the once-over. "Nice dodge of the question, but I'll take your answer as a compliment."

She would. Haley liked retaining power just as much as he did. She was a dominant woman, likely underestimated in her position at Black Crescent. Did they realize what a dynamic powerhouse they had in their possession? Because Chase had been with her only a few times and he could see that she deserved to be in a higher position, definitely higher pay. He had no clue what her financial status was, but she deserved more. Having someone like Haley on his team would be invaluable.

And he fully intended to have her on his team… and in his bed.

Two totally different scenarios, yes, but he wanted her in any way he could have her. Now he just had to figure out how the hell to make sure she didn't hate him when all of this was over, but even more than that, he had to find a way to make sure she wasn't hurt. That was the last thing he wanted in the end.

"You're staring."

Her statement pulled him back and he realized she was still looking at him over her shoulder.

"Maybe I like having you here and I just wanted to mentally capture the moment."

Haley turned fully to face him, crossing her arms over her chest and pursing her lips. "Do you practice those charming lines in the mirror each morning or are you that smooth by default?"

Unable to keep the distance another minute, Chase moved forward and closed the gap between them.

"Nothing to practice," he countered, reaching up to stroke the back of his hand along her jaw-line. "I see you and something just pulls me. I can't explain it."

Something came over her eyes, something other than desire. Guilt? Worry? He had a heavy dose of both himself, but those emotions had no place here. Not tonight.

"I can't explain it, either," she replied. "But I know what I want and I don't care about the rest of the outside forces right now."

Another way they were so alike. They both shared a passion for each other and they hadn't even removed their clothing yet. He couldn't wait to get her in his bed, to bring out that fire in her and have his fantasies fulfilled.

"Nothing is more attractive than a woman who knows what she wants." He reached around to toy with the ends of the tie on her jumpsuit. "Except maybe this outfit. Did you wear this to drive me crazy?"

"Perhaps. How did I do?"

He gave the tie a yank, sending the material floating down away from her breasts. Now, fully bare from the torso up, Haley merely stood before him with her eyes locked on his, clearly confident in her radiant beauty and sexuality.

"Damn good," he stated before he covered her mouth with his own.

Eight

Haley wrapped her arms around Chase's neck and arched her body into his. Was this really happening? Was she letting it?

Yes, and oh, hell yes.

Work didn't matter now. The CEO position didn't matter now. Those alarm bells going off in her head telling her why this was going to be a terrible idea in the long run didn't matter, either.

All that mattered was that she and Chase were both adults. Both very consenting adults who were going after what they wanted. She'd come here knowing full well what was going to happen. The promise of seeing that sunrise from his bed had been impossible to turn down.

But it was the anticipation of all the thrilling things between now and that sunrise that had her more than ready and willing to come home with Chase.

"I've wanted you here for weeks," he muttered against her lips. "I want to take my time, but I need you too bad."

The feeling was quite mutual. She didn't care if he moved fast or slow, she just wanted to get this going before the ache inside her became too overwhelming.

Chase's hands roamed up her bare back as he eased away and stared into her eyes, then that heavy-lidded gaze traveled down to her exposed chest.

The way he looked at her made her feel sexy, like she was the most beautiful woman he'd ever seen.

With a boldness she felt only with him, Haley reached for the buttons on his shirt and slid each one through the slot…one by one. He kept his eyes on hers as she revealed tanned skin and a dark smattering of chest hair. She parted his shirt and yanked it from his pants.

In a flurry of hands and an occasional laugh

when they fumbled, they had their clothes off and flung all around in a matter of moments.

Haley's heart beat so fast. She wasn't an innocent by any means, but there was something about Chase that made her want to remember this, that made her feel like something about this moment was special.

But it couldn't be. No. They were both playing a game of cat and mouse and she had no idea which position she was in...or maybe they kept trading off. Either way, this night was only about physical because there could be nothing more between them.

"If you're scowling, then I'm doing something wrong."

His words brought her back and she smiled.

"You're doing everything right," she told him, looping her arms around her neck. "And I'm assuming these windows are one-way?"

Chase nipped at her lips, then her chin, and traveled down the column of her neck. "Privacy is imperative to me."

He released her for just a moment before grabbing his pants and pulling out protection. In no time, Chase had himself covered, and he turned back to her with a hunger in his eyes that had her entire body heating up even more.

When he hoisted her up and plastered her back

against the glass, Haley shivered at the very idea that anyone could see them. Though she knew they couldn't, just the thrill of having Chase so out of control had her anticipation building even more.

"Tell me if you don't like anything," he murmured against her lips.

Haley locked her ankles behind his back and laced her fingers around his neck. "I won't like it if you keep talking."

He offered her a naughty grin as he joined their bodies. In an instant, everything around them vanished. Haley had been waiting for this moment, this man.

One hand gripped her hip and the other cleverly traveled over her bare skin. He touched her, kissed her, consumed her. Every part of this was so perfect.

Haley arched her body against his as Chase's lips landed on the swell of her breast. Between the expert jerk of his hips and those hands and lips, Haley let out a moan she could no longer suppress. She was done hiding her feelings, done ignoring what she wanted. For tonight, she would be herself.

She might not trust Chase with his business motives, but she wholeheartedly trusted him intimately...because he wanted the same thing from this that she did. A good time and no strings.

His fingertips tightened on her hip as he

pumped faster, his warm breath washing over her heated skin. Haley couldn't hold back her climax another second. The pleasure spiraled through her as her knees pressed into his sides. Chase captured her lips as his own body jerked and stilled.

She clung to him until her tremors ceased, and even then she wasn't ready to let go. She wasn't ready to face reality or harsh truths. She wanted to be selfish just a bit longer.

Chase eventually eased back, smoothing her hair away from her face as he stared down into her eyes. There was something she couldn't quite put her finger on, something almost remorseful in his gaze.

"Regrets already?" she asked, only half joking.

The muscle in Chase's jaw clenched as he shook his head. "I don't do regrets."

Well, that was good to know. She'd hate to think she was considered a mistake.

He slowly helped her get steady on her feet and Haley had a sudden sense of insecurity. She stood before him completely naked after having frenzied sex against a window.

What was the protocol now? Did she make a joke to take out some of the tension? Did she just get dressed like this was no big deal?

But this was a big deal. An extremely epic deal because she didn't do one-night stands. She didn't

do flings. She sure as hell never slept with someone who could become her boss.

He wasn't her boss yet, though.

"Regrets?" he asked, mimicking her earlier
question.

Haley threw him a glance as she went to gather
her clothing. "No regrets, just trying to figure out
what to say."

"You don't have to say anything," he told her,
clearly comfortable with his state of undress…
as he should be. "There are no rules here, Haley.
We're adults."

Yes, but there should be rules. Shouldn't there?

"I should go."

Haley quickly dressed. She figured staying
wasn't smart since this was just a fling.

As she adjusted the tie on her jumpsuit, Chase's
hand settled on the small of her back. Stilling beneath his touch, Haley threw him a glance over
her shoulder.

"Don't get lost in that head of yours," he told
her with a smile. "Despite what you might think
of me, I don't do this type of thing, either."

"And what thing is that?" she countered.
"Flings? Sleeping with someone to get ahead in
a job?"

As soon as the words were out of her mouth,
she regretted them. She was being bitchy because

she was confused and flustered. She still felt the tingling effects of their encounter and she was trying to sort all of this out, which was damn hard considering she still felt his touch.

"I'm sorry," she told him, turning to face him fully. "That was uncalled for."

Chase pushed her hair over her shoulders before framing her face and stepping to her. "Nothing to apologize for. But let's get one thing straight right now. When I land CEO, it won't be because we slept together. I wanted you. I want the job. The two have nothing to do with each other."

The confidence he exuded was so sexy. Everything about him was sexy, alluring, mesmerizing. Maybe that was why she was so confused about her feelings. Because she didn't do flings, she could easily see herself getting more wrapped up in this man, and that definitely would be a bad idea.

Chase slid his lips over hers. "Stay," he murmured. "No expectations. Just…stay."

As if she could refuse this man anything.

Haley wanted to stay, so she'd just have to figure out all the other stuff later.

After pouring Haley a glass of wine, Chase stepped out onto his balcony and crossed to the outdoor sitting area.

"This view never gets old," he said, handing her the glass. "It's always so peaceful and the perfect way to unwind after a long day."

She took the glass and curled her feet beneath her on the sofa. "I'd be tempted to sleep out here," she stated with a smile. "I'd definitely settle out here in my downtime with a good book."

Chase took a seat beside her, extending his arm along the back of the sofa as he shifted to face her.

"Downtime," he repeated with a chuckle. "Is that something you have?"

Haley sipped her wine and shrugged. "Lately? No. Josh pushes me to leave when he does or even take a day off, but there's just too much to be done."

Ah, yes. Josh. Let's talk about him.

"So your boss isn't demanding?" Chase asked. "All of this work is self-imposed?"

"Maybe a little of both," she corrected. "I demand enough of myself and take pride in my position. Josh and I used to really rub each other the wrong way when the transition was taking place and here and there over the years. He sees me as a little sister, and brothers and sisters argue."

Just like Chase thought…a bastard like his father. Haley was brilliant and anyone who couldn't identify that was a damn fool.

"It took a couple of years but he now sees me

as an equal." Haley laughed and took another sip of her wine. "Actually, he's come to see that I'm invaluable in my position and he's been asking my opinion on the new hire. He's a great guy and I'm happy for him for going after his dreams instead of staying out of duty. That's a fine line to hold on to. Love or loyalty."

Love. Chase wouldn't know about that, but loyalty…hell, yes. He was going through all of this out of loyalty to his family. To seek justice and secure redemption.

"You will be invaluable to me when I take over," he told her.

Her smile widened. "You're so sure this is going to happen for you."

"Because it is," he assured her. "I wouldn't have started if I thought I would fail."

"Do you fail at anything?" she asked.

He thought to when he couldn't save his family, when his father went to prison and his mother had a nervous breakdown.

"Only one time. I vowed to never let myself get that vulnerable again."

Haley finished her wine and set the glass on the table before settling back into the sofa. Her head dropped back against his arm, her eyes meeting his.

"What makes you want this job so bad?" she

asked. "You're successful already. You don't need the boost in your finances or ego…or maybe you do. I really don't know much about you."

Yet she'd slept with him and hadn't gone home. That just proved she was more invested in whatever was happening between them than he'd ever anticipated.

And maybe so was he. While he wasn't looking for any type of relationship, he couldn't ignore that he wanted her here, that he enjoyed her company even outside the bedroom. She challenged him, made him smile during a time when he'd been so hell-bent on revenge. She was refreshing at a time when he didn't know happiness or distractions were even possible.

"Finances aren't an issue," he agreed carefully. "I'm always looking for ways to grow and better myself. Black Crescent is the perfect next step in my life."

"Because of that whole family thing," she reminded him with a smile. "And what happens if you don't get the position?"

Chase couldn't help but laugh. "You're not a great motivational speaker, you know."

Haley's smile tugged at him… Everything about her seemed to pull him little by little closer to her world. It wasn't her world he'd set out to infiltrate, yet here he was spending more and more time with her and slowly being pulled away from his ultimate goal.

"Listen, I'm not the final decision-maker," she explained as she leaned closer. "I also shouldn't even be discussing this position outside of work. Not only is it unprofessional, it is disrespectful to Josh."

Yes, Josh. The golden boy. Well, Chase had been doing some digging on Josh. It was best to find out any hidden secrets and dirty details when taking down an opponent. Besides the whole replacement aspect he was working on, Chase also heard rumors that Josh had fathered another woman's baby...not his fiancée's.

Granted, Josh wasn't the one who had destroyed Chase's family, but the guy had swooped in and taken over his crooked father's company. There had to be some semblance of Vernon Lowell in the son who was so take-charge. Chase hadn't wasted his time digging into the other brothers' pasts, though it would be impossible to ignore the rumors that surrounded Oliver and his heavy addiction.

Chase leaned closer to Haley and rested his hand on her upper thigh. "You're invaluable to your company and I don't want you discussing anything you're not comfortable with."

Haley settled her hand over his and smiled. "It's

not my company. If you ask my parents, I'm just an assistant. I'm pretty sure they think I sharpen pencils and make coffee all day."

More than once she'd mentioned her parents and their lack of respect for not only her, but also her critical role at Black Crescent.

"Have you ever told them your worth to the company?" he asked. Forget the fact she should be invaluable to her own parents as a remarkable daughter.

Haley let out a humorless laugh. "It's really not worth the fight. I struggled for good grades in school. I had to work my butt off for Bs and Cs. So they naturally dismissed me from growing up to be successful."

"Naturally?" he questioned, trying to tamp down his rage. "That's not natural parenting, Haley. Some kids work harder than others and some just have an easier time. That doesn't mean you can't be successful."

"Yes, well, I'm used to it and actually over it." She eased closer and slid her hand around his neck. "Let's not talk about them anymore."

That desire flashed back into her eyes, and if it was a distraction she needed, then so be it. He didn't mind being used by Haley to keep her mind off unpleasant things. Besides, he shouldn't want to get that personal with her anyway, right?

Yet he couldn't help himself.

Tonight he would take what he wanted, in return keeping Haley's thoughts solely on him. Tomorrow he would go back to trying to pry deeper into the company via her mind.

The end was in sight, and he was too close to having it all to turn back now.

Nine

"No, Mom. I'm fine."

Chase assured his mother once again. He couldn't be angry at her for consistently asking. The woman was worried about her son taking on the family that nearly destroyed them.

He clutched his cell and turned away from his desk to face the large picture window.

"I promise, I'm careful," he assured her as he glanced out onto the river.

The sun shone high in the sky and Haley had gone home after breakfast…which he'd served in bed. Last night had been a turning point, though he still wasn't quite sure which direction he was actually pointing to at the moment.

"I can't help but be concerned," she told him. "I hope you aren't making a mistake."

"Life doesn't come with guarantees, but I didn't set out to lose," he stated. "I know what I'm doing with Black Crescent."

With Haley, though, not so much. Oh, they'd had a hell of a good time last night, but he had no idea where this would go. If they'd gotten together under much different circumstances, Chase wouldn't mind seeing where this could lead. Considering he wasn't being completely honest with her, and that he wanted to bring down her beloved boss, Chase knew this fling could only be temporary at best.

"Promise that you'll check in so I don't worry."

Chase smiled. "I promise. There's nothing for you to worry about."

Once he finished the call, Chase held his cell at his side and pulled in a deep breath. While he always loved talking to his mother, he'd been waiting on his private detective to call this morning. He had been doing some deeper digging into Josh Lowell's past and Chase needed as much information as he could get if he was ultimately going to slide into that CEO position.

Haley was proving to continually be the ever-loyal employee and was not letting much slip. His plan had been to spend more time with her, to get her to somehow unknowingly let slide tidbits of information about the company, but she was still so close-lipped. If anything, she only sang Josh's praises and the company's as a whole. She'd been there during the fallout, so there was no way she wasn't fully aware of every dirty deed that went down. Not everything was public and it was those insider details he needed to uncover.

His cell vibrated in his hand. Chase glanced to the screen and saw the call he'd been waiting on. Maybe now he would get that ammunition he needed to secure his spot at Black Crescent and take down the Lowells once and for all.

Matteo Velez sat across from her desk and waited for his interview time. Haley watched as he went from checking his phone to glancing around the room. He seemed distracted, like something more important occupied his thoughts.

More important than an interview for the CEO position? That seemed quite off and extremely unprofessional.

Did he even want to be here?

The handsome businessman would certainly be a sexy replacement for her current boss, but Haley still had her sights set on another mogul.

While Matt may be a head-turner with that dark suit and his intense stare, he wasn't the one who had her questioning her sanity and getting lost in thought during working hours.

No, that privilege belonged to the mysterious Chase Hargrove.

Josh stepped from his office and caught Haley's eyes, pulling her from her thoughts and back to the moment and the interview.

"Matt," Josh stated, turning his attention to the latest applicant. "I hope I didn't keep you waiting."

Coming to his feet, Matt shook his head and buttoned his suit jacket. "No problem at all. I'm thankful I managed a second interview."

"You deserve it," Josh corrected. "With a résumé like the one you have, you are already high up on the list."

Matt nodded. Haley found it odd that he didn't smile or seem thrilled at the prospect of being the next CEO. What was going on with this guy?

"My assistant, Haley, will again be sitting in on the interview," Josh said, gesturing to her. "She's been with Black Crescent the longest and she will be your greatest asset to the company."

Matt flashed her a grin. "The right-hand woman," he stated. "There's always one major player in any company who remains behind the scenes and works the long hours."

Haley laughed. "I'd say the long hours are a toss-up between Josh and me, but yes. I do love my job and whoever takes over this position will be working closely with me."

"Let's step into my office. Allison couldn't be here in person, but I have her on conference call."

Josh gestured to the open door behind him and let Haley step in first. She wasn't so sure that Matt had the truest of intentions. He didn't seem overly thrilled to be here, which could always be just nerves or anticipation. He could be a man who just held his emotions close to his chest.

He could also have ulterior motives like Chase. And if that was the case, then Haley had more work cut out for her. She'd never considered the applicants might have past issues with Josh's father or the family in general. It was fifteen years ago. Did people even hold grudges that long?

That was certainly something she needed to take into account. If she came up with too many red flags, she'd have to meet with Josh and express her concerns. Vernon had certainly destroyed quite a few families so it wasn't beyond the realm of possibility for those kids to now want revenge.

Haley settled into her seat and listened as Josh and Allison conducted the interview. Every now and then she interjected and asked her own questions, impressed by Matt's answers.

Maybe Matt should be in the running, but part of her wondered how she would feel if the position went to Chase…and how she would feel if it didn't.

The time was drawing near when a decision would be made and she would have to adjust no matter what the outcome.

All the more reason for her to follow up with that investigator she'd contacted Saturday afternoon about digging into Chase's past and the past of his parents.

There was more to the story than what she'd uncovered on her own and she wouldn't rest until she discovered the full truth of the man she was falling for.

"So you're telling me you finished your schooling in half the time?"

Just when he thought she couldn't get any more amazing, Haley threw out another fact from her past.

"I buckled down and wanted to be done," she told him as she propped her feet on his lap. "I still lived at home and working as an intern gave me enough to save so the second I graduated, I had enough to get my first apartment and a cheap car."

No wonder she was so loyal. Black Crescent and Vernon Lowell had given her a break and taken a chance. Likely they had been her haven when she wanted and needed to be appreciated and probably loved in a way she hadn't been before.

Ironic that's what she'd found in a company run by a scoundrel, but Vernon did different things for different people apparently. Or maybe Josh had taken on the new intern. Chase didn't know the dynamics there, and he'd be jealous if he wasn't sure Josh thought of Haley as a sister.

Chase slid his hand over Haley's delicate ankles. He'd coerced her into coming for dinner, where he'd prepared everything himself. He'd given his chef the night off again so he and Haley could have complete privacy.

Even Al had been given the night off from any duties. The less his well-meaning father figure/ driver/shoulder to lean on knew the better.

"Where did you learn to cook like that?" she asked, resting her head against the back of the sofa and offering him a lazy smile. "I know they don't teach you how to whip potatoes on the football field."

"No. No, they don't," he laughed in agreement. "My mother is an amazing cook and she taught me a few things. Others I've learned on my own through trial and error. I do have a chef for various events and when I have company, but I wanted tonight to just be about us."

Her eyes held his, her smile slowly fading away. "Is there an *us*?"

"Whatever is happening here constitutes as an *us*." His hand slid higher on her leg, but he kept his eyes locked on hers. "Let's not look any further than this."

"*This* as in sex?"

Her bold question had him smiling as his thumb grazed over the curve of her knee. "We're both too married to our careers to worry about anything else right now."

Her legs shifted as she nestled deeper into the sofa, her eyes drawing heavier in that sexy, bedroom-glare type of way—the way that did absolutely nothing to hide the hunger and the desire she possessed.

The idea of her sharing that passion with another man set off a wave of jealousy he hadn't experienced with another woman. Part of him wondered if he'd just gotten in too deep with her, if their relatable backgrounds and drive for business made her seem like the perfect woman.

"People like us?" she repeated. "You told me you wanted a family."

"I do," he affirmed, his hand now splayed across her thigh. "But right now, I have other goals in mind."

Her gaze dropped to his mouth, then back up

to his eyes. "We're not talking about the CEO position anymore."

"We're not talking anymore at all."

He inched up her body, his hands taking the hem of her little sundress higher, as well. He wasn't ready to talk, wasn't ready to look into all the messed-up emotions rolling through his mind.

Part of him wanted to know what would have happened had he met Haley under different circumstances. Part of him wanted to know what his mother would have thought of Haley. No doubt they would've gotten along…if Chase had let such a meeting take place.

But that was all a ridiculous line of thinking and a dangerous path to take at this stage in the game.

Haley arched against him, letting out a soft moan as her lids fluttered closed. That reaction was exactly what he wanted. Having her beneath him, ready to join together in the most primal, intimate way, was more than he'd ever thought when he'd first met her. He might not know what the hell he was doing in the long run with her, but he wasn't looking at anything beyond tonight. He couldn't even think about that or the guilt would overcome him.

Chase gripped her hips and jerked her beneath him even more as he settled between her legs. Her eyes shot up to his as a wicked smile spread across her face.

When she opened her mouth, Chase covered it with his own. He really didn't want to talk now and he was afraid of what she'd say. Communicating through their bodies seemed the safest way... at least for now.

Without words, Chase slid her panties down her legs, quickly rid himself of his pants, found protection and settled exactly where he wanted to be. And, if her moans and soft cries were any indicators, this was exactly where she wanted him to be.

Resting his elbows on either side of her head, Chase smoothed her hair from her face and made sure to keep his focus solely on her as he joined their bodies. Haley's ankles came around to lock behind his back, urging him deeper.

When her eyes connected with his, Chase stilled. There was some underlying emotion staring back at him, one he couldn't afford to dig into and one that would likely scare the hell out of him.

Closing his eyes might be the coward's way out, but there was no other option...not now.

Haley threaded her fingers through his hair, tugging ever so slightly. Chase rose up, gripping her hips as he went. Looking down at her with her hair a mess over his sofa, her dress bunched around her waist and her breathing coming out in short bursts had him quickening the pace.

There was something so addicting about this woman and until he found out how to break this cycle, he was damn well going to hang on for the ride.

"Chase."

The whispered word that slipped through her lips as her body tightened all around him had Chase reaching his own peak. Pleasure tore through him, his fingertips dug into her hips and Chase let himself go. Haley continued to whisper his name over and over. He found himself wrapped in her arms and legs, and he wondered how he'd been looming over her and was now being cradled by her warmth, her...

No. Not her love. Love didn't belong here and he sure as hell didn't want it.

As he lay half on, half off her heated body, Chase knew reality would hit sooner rather than later. At some point, he would have to complete his revenge and keep Haley out of the path of destruction in the process.

Ten

Haley stepped inside her front door and immediately slipped out of her heels. She'd been running around all day and had barely even sat at her desk. Between the ongoing interviews with Josh and CEO prospects and running to Tomorrow's Leaders to greet the newest recipients, Haley's feet were killing her.

She'd also missed lunch and the time had well passed any normal dinner schedule. Perhaps she should just pop open a bottle of Pinot and relax in a hot bubble bath. She definitely hadn't taken enough personal time lately with all the spare time she'd been spending with Chase.

Not that she was at all sorry. Her feelings for him were growing each time they were together. Granted, intimacy had a tendency to force people together at least in an emotional manner. Haley didn't do flings and she didn't take sex lightly. If she hadn't had some deeper pull toward Chase, she never would have slept with him.

She hadn't seen him since she'd left his house the other night after he'd blown her mind on his living room couch. They'd texted, but they'd both been busy with work… At least she assumed that's what he'd been busy with.

Haley bent to retrieve her shoes as she made her way toward her master suite. The next thing to go after the shoes was always the bra. She was so done with this day. While she'd accomplished quite a bit, she had run out of steam.

Her cell chimed in the purse she still had over her shoulder. With a groan, she stepped into her room and tossed her purse onto her bed before digging out her phone.

Marcus's name lit up her screen. With a sigh, she swiped the screen and made her way into her adjoining bath.

"I just left you," she said in lieu of a hello. "Is something wrong?"

"Not at all," Marcus replied. "In fact, everything is rather amazing. We had an anonymous donor just give enough to cover all of the textbooks for each of the new recipients starting college in the fall. The amount also covers anything else they may need as far as laptops, notebooks and individual class fees. There's also a buffer amount for anything that may have been overlooked."

Stunned, Haley turned and sank down onto the edge of her bed. "Who paid for all of that?"

"The money came in electronically with a detailed note of what to purchase for the incoming students," Marcus explained. "There was also a message stating that there would be more donations at the beginning of each quarter for new classes. But honestly, that padded amount that's left would more than cover an entire year. I don't know who this guy is, but he's certainly invested in Tomorrow's Leaders. I mean, I'm glad, but I wish we knew who to thank properly."

Yeah, she did, too, but she also had a good idea who would suddenly be invested in her beloved charity. Not that she would divulge that information to anyone, not even her right-hand man.

"Well, let's just be thankful," she replied. "It's not like we haven't had anonymous donors before. We just typically don't have such specific notes."

"I know you would've seen the email, but I wanted to give you a heads-up," Marcus told her.

"Go about your evening. I'm sure you were about ready to dive into a much-needed bottle of wine."

Haley laughed as she turned the knobs on her large soaker tub. She grabbed a bottle on the edge and dumped a hefty dose of lavender bubble bath in.

"You know me so well."

"I know you don't take enough time for yourself, so go enjoy. I'm sure I'll talk to you tomorrow."

"Thanks, Marcus. Good night."

She disconnected the call and stripped out of her clothes. After grabbing her kimono off the back of the bathroom door, she headed to the kitchen to get that glass of wine while her tub filled with hot, bubbly water.

Chase and his wily ways had her smiling. He thought he was sneaky—or perhaps he didn't. Maybe he'd fully intended for her to figure out who had deposited such a large sum.

Oh, sure, someone else could've left that deposit with a detailed email, but she didn't think so. He'd been impressed with her charity and had been eager to help.

Moments later, Haley padded back through her house and into her bathroom. The suds filled the white bathtub and the aroma instantly relaxed her. She set her stemless glass on the edge and slid the knot from her tie. The kimono landed on the floor as Haley stepped into the warm water.

She sank down, letting the bubbles consume her. Her glass and cell sat beside her, but she closed her eyes and dropped her head against her bath pillow. For just a moment, she wanted to lie here and do absolutely nothing.

Okay, maybe she wanted to think about Chase and those damn gestures that made her like him even more. Maybe she wanted to reach out to him and call him out on it. If nothing else, she did want to tell him thank you. She didn't have to make a big deal about thanking him and she didn't plan on embarrassing him, but she did want him to know how much she appreciated what he'd done.

Her cell vibrated again and she peeked out of one eye to the screen. Emails. Always emails.

Another vibration had her screen lighting up with a text from the PI she had digging a little deeper into Chase's parents.

Her curiosity got the best of her and she reached with her dry hand and swiped the screen. The text told her she might want to check her emails ASAP.

Urgency had her tapping on the email icon and opening the message. Haley wanted to take in the entire email at once, so her eyes scanned over all the bullet points before she went back and read each word at a slower pace. Her heart clenched at the information revealed, the ache in the pit of her stomach gnawing as she read very plausible motivations for Chase's urgent desire to take over Black Crescent Hedge Fund.

His father had been incarcerated after a paper trail from the company and Vernon forced the police to take action. She'd known Chase's father had also been part of the embezzling, but she hadn't been sure as to what extent. According to the email, he had been a minor player in the game, but Vernon's well-laid trail led straight to Dale's door.

She read on, finding that his mother was institutionalized after she'd had a nervous breakdown, just like Haley had originally thought. Their family home had been foreclosed after his father went to prison and then his mother had fallen ill. Once his mother was hospitalized, Chase was left alone. No wonder that football scholarship had been so important. That's all he'd had left—his sport and his education.

Is that why he wanted to help her organization so much? To give kids a chance when they wouldn't otherwise have one?

She also read where he'd changed his name right after his mother had been sent for psychiatric help. He'd legally done so and the patterns from then on showed a timeline in black-and-white of Chase working toward revenge on Black Crescent and the Lowell family.

Haley swallowed as a burning sensation pricked her eyes and the back of her throat. He'd been angry for years, so angry he'd changed his major from education to business and graduated in record time… something he'd failed to mention when they'd been discussing her accomplishments.

Setting her phone back on the edge of the bathtub, Haley grabbed her wine. Sipping was out. Gulping was necessary now.

Clearly he'd been planning on trying to infiltrate Black Crescent. Had he been waiting for the CEO position to open up? There was no way he would've known that Josh wanted out because initially Josh had planned to stay. Granted, being a business mogul hadn't been Josh's first choice. He did put his family first and had done everything to rebuild the family name.

Yet now that he'd fallen in love with Sophie and the two were planning a life together, Josh decided to pursue art, his true passion. Haley couldn't blame him. After all, he'd put his life on hold when his brothers didn't want to step up…or in Oliver's case of addiction, he couldn't step up.

Haley knew Oliver was doing better, had put that hellish time behind him, but he still wasn't up to taking over a corporation the magnitude of Black Crescent.

Finishing off her wine, Haley settled back against the cushy pillow and let all of this information roll through her mind. As much as she wanted to confront Chase and find the answers to her questions—mainly wanting to know if she'd been part of the plan all along—Haley knew she had to be patient and take her time here. There was too much at stake...namely her heart, but also the integrity and future of the company.

If Chase ended up as CEO, what would he do to the place that Haley basically called home? What would happen to all the employees who were loyal to Josh? Not to mention the elite customers they dealt with. Wouldn't taking down Black Crescent just be déjà vu of what happened years ago with Vernon?

Haley didn't like lies, betrayal or deceit. She prided herself on honesty and transparency, but she also prided herself on her strength and ability to withstand the toughest of situations.

There was only one way to find out what Chase's true motives were, and she was going to have to go against everything she valued and held dear.

Haley was going to have to turn a blind eye to her honesty and set a trap for Chase...all the while pretending everything between them was perfectly fine. In truth, the dynamics had completely changed. Her emotional involvement had already surpassed anything she'd expected or even wanted.

While she had no clue what would happen next or how her plan would play out, Haley was certain of one thing… Someone was going to get hurt.

Eleven

Chase wasn't at all surprised that Haley reciprocated the dinner idea and invited him to her place. There was something stirring between them, something that had nothing to do with his revenge plot or his career.

He genuinely liked her, wanted to spend more time with her. That caring side of her had him wondering how she could ever have stayed loyal to a company run by such a bastard. For someone so loving and giving of herself to others, she'd started working at a young age for the exact opposite type of personality.

On the positive side of things, Vernon had left before he could corrupt Haley. Chase hated to think what that man would've done to someone as innocent and generous as Haley.

With a firm hold on the raspberry torte he'd made, Chase rang Haley's doorbell and stepped back to wait.

Seconds later, the door swung wide, revealing a stunning hostess. Her hair tumbled over her shoulders and the little red dress she wore left absolutely nothing to the imagination, stopping high on her thigh and with a deep V in the front. The woman was already driving him crazy…and from the naughty smile, she knew exactly what game she was playing.

Damn his hormones and her for making him live in a constant state of arousal and need.

"Perfect timing," she told him. "I just took the dishes out of the oven."

Her eyes darted to the dish in his hands, then back up to his face.

"Did you throw the box away and put your dessert in that fancy dish just for me?"

Chase scoffed. "A box? I'll have you know I made this with my own two hands. I didn't buy it and I didn't even have my chef make it."

Haley's brows rose as she stepped back and gestured for him to come inside. "Why don't you tell me how you know how to make such a decadent-looking dessert over dinner."

She turned from the door and sashayed back into her home. Chase's gaze instantly fell to those swaying hips as he followed her, closing the door at his back.

The spacious open concept offered him an even bigger glimpse into her life. Simplistic furniture in pale grays in contrast against dark flooring but pops of colors in greenery from plants and bright throw pillows really pulled in both sides of Haley. The career woman in Haley always had a polished, conservative look. But that inner vixen and good-time girl came out to play once business hours were over.

The more he uncovered about this woman, the more he wished like hell they could have met under very different circumstances.

Haley busied herself scooping dinner onto plates and then she poured two glasses of red wine. She hummed a soft tune he didn't recognize but that he instantly found relaxing.

"My mother always hummed." The thought hit him and just tumbled out before he could stop himself. Interestingly enough, he found that he wanted to share more about his past with her. "When I was younger, she would always hum 'You Are My

Sunshine.' Cooking dinner, folding laundry, that was just her song."

Haley stared across the long kitchen island and offered one of her sweet smiles. "You don't talk much about your parents. That's a beautiful memory."

His parents meant everything to him and while they certainly had their difficult times—some had seemed so bleak and dire—they always had each other. He and his mom and dad never lacked love or loyalty.

That was the entire reason he was here today. That path he'd started years ago led him to Haley. Guilt grew more and more each day. What started out as rage and anger had turned to desire and passion.

"Everything okay?"

Haley's concerned question pulled Chase back to the moment. He nodded and grinned.

"Fine," he assured her. "What can I do to help?"

She continued to stare, her brows drawn in worry. Chase didn't want to get into the mess going on inside his mind, and even his heart. While he did a damn good job of keeping his heart protected, that didn't mean he was a complete bastard. He cared for Haley, there was no denying that, but he also still had a job to do…literally.

He hadn't come this far in his life, in his plans,

to get sidelined by hormones and an innocent woman who had him questioning everything.

When she continued to stare, Chase came around the island and picked up the plates. "Where to?"

He waited, hoping she wouldn't pry any deeper into his past. There was nothing more he could reveal without giving away who he truly was and what he was doing centering himself into her life.

"Let's go out on the balcony," she finally stated. "It's such a nice night."

She led the way through the living room and out onto the spacious balcony overlooking a sloped backyard with a small pond and fountain. Such a simple space, but so perfect for Haley. She had a beautiful home in an upscale part of town and she didn't have to tell him that everything she had, she'd worked her ass off for. No one had helped her, least of all her family. All of her accomplishments were only because this woman had drive and determination and wouldn't let anyone stand in her way.

And that right there was so damn sexy, he couldn't even deny that she was quite possibly the most perfect woman he'd ever met.

Too bad she could never be his.

"Oh, do you care to go into the dining area and

grab the napkin holder from the table?" she asked. "I'll go get the utensils."

"Sure."

Chase stepped back into her house and passed through the living area to the small dining room. Spread across the table were papers, which caught his attention with the Black Crescent Hedge Fund logo on several documents. The napkin holder was nowhere to be seen on the table, but the highlighters he'd brought her were lying in a bundle on the side.

As much as he wanted to glance through those papers, he couldn't. A month ago, if given this opportunity, he'd sure as hell have taken advantage, but now... Well, everything had changed.

"Damn it," he muttered as he turned to glance around the room.

The sideboard had a decorative napkin holder full of napkins. Chase grabbed it and started to head out, but not before one last longing glance at the papers. Josh's signature was scrawled across the bottom of a few documents, but Chase ignored his curiosity.

Now wasn't the time to betray Haley's trust. He vowed to himself not to let her get hurt. He would do everything he could to prevent Haley from getting caught in the middle of this twisted web.

Walking away from those papers was the most

difficult thing he'd done in a while. Maybe they wouldn't have shed any light on his master plan, but there was a possibility they would have.

What should he have done, though? Stood there sorting through the piles, or perhaps pulled out his cell and started snapping pics so he could look over them in his private time? And do all of that while Haley waited for him on the balcony for a romantic dinner? Only a complete jerk would do such a thing.

When he stepped back out onto the balcony, he saw that Haley had lit two small candles and had arranged a colorful bundle of flowers in a simple glass vase between their plates. She held her arms out, gesturing toward the table.

"Ta-da."

Chase laughed. "Is that why you had me step away?"

She shrugged and pulled the chair out for him. "I just wanted to do something nice. I mean, it's no bouquet of highlighters or homemade raspberry torte, but…"

Chase couldn't remember the last time someone did something for him. Not something that didn't have to do with business or using him to get ahead. Haley had no reason to use him, no reason to play him. No, in all of this he was the one using, and that damn weight kept mounting on his shoulders… Soon the heaviness would become too much to bear.

This sweet gesture of dinner and a romantic ambiance put a vise around his heart and he'd done so well in keeping his heart out of this equation so far.

Chase set the napkins on the table and turned to face her. That punch of lust he always experienced when he looked at her now layered with something else…something deeper, more meaningful, but definitely something he couldn't label.

Honestly, he didn't want to put a label on any of this because that would hint dangerously close to a relationship.

But physical, that was something he could grasp and control. It was an emotion, a reaction he knew.

Reaching for her, Chase curled his fingers around that dip in her waist and pulled her closer.

"This is all amazing," he told her, leaning in. "The dinner, the atmosphere, sexy dress. You didn't have to do all of this for me."

Her smile widened as she looped her arms around his neck. "Maybe I did it for us. Maybe I like spending time with you and I wanted to look nice even though we're staying in."

Hell yes they were staying in. There was no way he was taking her out because he wasn't sure how long he'd be able to control himself. Peeling her out of that dress had just jumped to the top of his priority list…even above those papers in the other room.

"Staying in is the best idea I've heard all day." He nipped at her lips, holding her hips flush against his own. "Did you wear this dress to drive me out of my mind?"

She tipped back, laughter dancing in her eyes. "Is it working?"

"You're lucky we've made it this long with our clothes still intact."

Haley framed his face and laid a quick kiss on his lips. "Dinner first. Then we can discuss dessert options."

She stepped from his hold and gestured to the chair she'd pulled out for him. "Sit and eat before it gets cold."

Reluctantly, he took a seat. "If this is some sort of foreplay, you're winning."

She reached for a napkin and snapped it open, then laid it in her lap. "I never lose," she promised with a leveled gaze.

As if he needed another reason to find her even more irresistible. But he needed to focus. Those papers and her sweetness layered with a heavy dose of sex appeal had really thrown him. He wasn't about to mention the papers, though. Likely she'd brought work home, and that certainly didn't surprise him.

Haley picked up her fork and speared a piece of beef. "So, tell me all about how you came to make amazing-looking desserts."

"Oh, they don't just look amazing, they taste incredible."

"Just add humble to your list of attributes."

Chase took a bite of what tasted like home-made noodles. "Humble has no space in my life. Confidence and risks have taken me everywhere I need to be."

"Please, no work talk," she begged. "I already had to bring home some forms to sort out and I just want one evening of doing absolutely nothing."

Chase set his fork down and reached across the small round table. "I'm glad you're taking some time for yourself."

"With you."

Chase raised his brows. "Is there someone else?"

"Oh, yes," she laughed. "I've been seeing all of the CEO applicants on the side. You know, just so I can see who I'm most compatible with."

He couldn't help but smile. A snarky comeback was another quality he appreciated.

"I deserved that," he told her. "When was the last time you dated before me?"

"Are we dating?" she asked.

The idea didn't bother him. What bothered him was the fact all of this was temporary. There was no long term here, even if he had the time to start feeding into a serious relationship.

"I'm exclusively sleeping with you and we've been out," he countered. "What do you want to call that?"

Haley pursed her lips as she reached for her wine. Swirling the contents, she leaned back in her chair and kept her focus on him.

"I'm not sure," she finally answered. "I like seeing you, I like sleeping with you and I don't want to do that with anyone else right now."

Right now. Did that mean she also thought this was temporary? Because the only reason he wasn't pursuing more was because he knew she would never forgive him for going after her beloved company.

So what was her reasoning for thinking this wouldn't grow into more?

And why the hell was he offended?

"So, about that torte," she went on. "Care to tell me how you came to that and are there any more hidden secrets you want to share?"

Hidden secrets? She wasn't ready to hear those,

though he knew they would come out eventually. With the position he currently was in, he just had to make sure she didn't hate him and understood his reasoning for his actions once this was all said and done.

Twelve

Haley rolled over, her hand reaching for Chase, only to find the spot not only empty but also cold.

Confused, she sat up in bed and glanced around the darkened room. A sliver from the hallway light filtered in.

After dinner, she and Chase had enjoyed more wine and a brief chat on the balcony. It didn't take long for them to move inside for some much needed privacy. They barely made it to the living room before their clothes were shed. Once that frenzied sex had taken place, Chase had carried her in the most romantic way possible to the bedroom, where they'd taken their time exploring each other.

So where was he now? She'd fallen asleep in his arms, nestled right against all of his strength and warmth.

The papers. Damn it. She'd left those out as part of her initial trap or plan or whatever the hell game she was playing in an attempt to test Chase's loyalty. She'd actually forgotten all about them once they'd started dinner. Of course, she'd sent him into the dining room to find her scattered mess. She'd purposely left the napkins in there, needing to get his curiosity pumping.

The papers she'd left out were actually private, but nothing that would harm the company. They did hold information that only she knew; not even Josh was aware of some of the contents. So if anything was leaked, there would be only one source.

Guilt curled low in her belly as she pushed the sheet aside. Swinging her legs over the side of the bed, she sat for just a moment and wondered what she should do now. She didn't like playing games, but she had to know where Chase really stood. Did he indeed want the CEO position or did he just want to destroy the company from within?

Did he want to destroy her in the process? Had she been part of his plan all along?

Fear spiraled through her, layering with the

guilt and the worry. If he wasn't playing her, then she hated how she'd tried to set a trap. But she had to protect not only herself, but also Black Crescent and everyone in their employ.

Haley came to her feet and grabbed her kimono from the antique trunk at the end of her bed. After sliding into it and securing the tie, she padded out into the hall. The decorative clock on the wall showed just after five in the morning. Considering this was a Sunday and not a typical workday, she'd like to have slept in a little longer in the arms of the man she was falling for.

Falling for and possibly being deceived by.

Mercy, this was starting to become a serious mess.

Haley stepped into the open living area where she saw Chase in the kitchen, standing over her coffeepot.

Wearing a dark suit certainly made Chase Hargrove drop-dead sexy, but having him in her kitchen wearing nothing but black boxer briefs and a mop of bedhead was a whole new side of sex appeal.

Haley couldn't examine too deeply just how having Chase in her home made her feel. Inviting a man into her personal space wasn't something she did, but she'd needed to set the trap.

Ugh. Even those words floating through her

mind made her nauseated. But thinking he was using her, that he might have gone into her dining area and leaked information about Black Crescent, made her feel even worse.

She shuffled her feet across the wood floor, causing Chase to turn. He offered her a crooked grin and raked a hand down his chest.

"Did I wake you?" he asked.

Haley shook her head. "I rolled over and you were gone."

"I'm an early riser."

Or maybe he wanted to catch her while she was asleep and rifle through her things? How long had he been alone in her home? Had he taken photos of the documents and already called his assistant or his family? Were his parents backing him?

She had way too many questions about the man standing practically naked in her kitchen.

Chase turned back to her coffee maker and sighed. He tapped a button, tapped another and shrugged.

"I was trying to figure out how to make coffee in this damn pot of yours, but there's only so far my degrees can take me."

Haley laughed, making her way around the bar island separating the living area from the kitchen. She stepped in beside him and glanced to the water, then the mess of coffee grounds he'd made on her counter.

"Well, it certainly helps to get the grounds into the filter," she stated. "Why don't you go have a seat and I'll do the coffee?"

He threw a heavy-lidded glance over his shoulder. "Is it because I've made a mess? I was going to clean that up, you know."

Haley patted his cheek. "I'm sure you were, but I can't stand chaos and this is already making my eye twitch."

Chase nodded and took a step to the side. "At least show me how to use this damn thing for next time."

Haley stilled, her attention going from the messy counter to the messy relationship.

"Next time?" she asked. "How often do you plan on staying over?"

Chase reached out and gave a slight tug on the tie of her kimono. "As often as you'll let me."

In a perfect world and under much different circumstances, she'd want nothing more than to have this man in her bed each night. She could think of no other way she'd like to fall asleep.

Unfortunately, she was almost positive she couldn't trust him and she had convinced herself that he was playing her…which meant she needed

to stay at least one step ahead of him until she uncovered the real truth.

An uncomfortable heaviness settled deep within
her. She needed space. She couldn't stand here next
to him, both of them wearing very little, with all of
these emotions. There was too much to consider,
too much to worry about and contemplate.

With a smile, Haley faced him. "Let me handle
the coffee. Go back to bed and I'll meet you there."

He leaned in, covered her mouth with his and
caught her so off guard she had to grip his bare
shoulders to keep upright. He released her just as
quickly and took a step back.

Haley reached for the edge of the counter to
maintain her balance as Chase headed back toward the bedroom. She waited until he disappeared
down the hallway and into the master suite.

Blowing out a breath she hadn't realized she'd
been holding, Haley closed her eyes and gathered
herself. After she cleaned up the coffee grounds
and got the brew going, she glanced toward the
hallway once more before going to the dining area.

The light from the kitchen illuminated into the
space and onto the table. The papers were exactly
how she'd had them. Not one had been moved, and
even though they looked like a mess, she knew in
what order they had been placed.

Was he not using her? He'd had the perfect opportunity to look over these documents and she was pretty positive he hadn't done a thing.

The sound of the coffeepot coming to the end of the cycle pulled her away from the table. Her plan worked, or didn't work, depending on how she wanted to look at things. He knew these pieces were here, so if he'd truly been out to sabotage her or the company, wouldn't he have moved them around to read them or snap pictures?

What if he was in this only for her?

But then if that was the case, what happened if he was hired and became her boss? Then what would people think? The staff knew Haley had sat in on the interviews. Would they think she'd chosen him because he slept with her?

Haley tried to push aside all the questions as she made her way back to the coffee. Chase waited on her in her room, and now that she knew his intentions might be real and honest, she couldn't wait to spend the morning with him and maybe see where all of this could lead.

"I have some more information."

Chase steered his SUV through the streets of downtown and listened as his personal investigator gave the details Chase had been waiting on.

"The information wasn't easy to come by and it's certainly going to cost you."

Chase rolled his eyes. The guy was the best in the business, but his ego seriously grated on Chase's last nerve. He wasn't in the mood for games. He just wanted the scoop he was paying for.

"What did you find?" Chase demanded as he came to a stoplight.

"The doctor that delivered the love child that is rumored to belong to Josh might have been a bit shady and untrustworthy…as was the mother of the child."

"How shady are we talking?"

"The doctor or the mother?"

Chase gripped the wheel and prayed for patience. "I want to know everything you found."

"Well, the doctor had been known to falsify a few birth certificates in his day," the investigator replied. "Hundreds if not thousands, in fact. He also manually changed DNA results once they were processed for a nice sum from his desperate clients. He practiced for over thirty years before he was caught and he's now incarcerated."

Interesting. The shady doctor working for a shady family. How quaint.

"The results also mention that the father could be Josh or his twin brother, Jake."

Well, at least that was something.

"And the more I dug into Josh's past, the more I found he's actually an upstanding guy. Nothing at all like his father. The guy seems to just want out of the family business, and I can hardly blame him. It has to be hell having the black cloud of Vernon Lowell hanging over your head your entire life."

"Send me over everything you found," Chase told him. "I need to see a few things for myself. I've already sent your payment, plus an extra bonus since you worked so hard."

Stroking that overinflated ego kept his investigator loyal and quiet. Those were two main qualities Chase demanded.

He disconnected the call with a tap to the screen on his dashboard. Instantly, music filled the vehicle and he cranked the metal up. He needed to think and when things were silent was when he nearly went out of his mind.

The light changed and Chase turned to take the familiar route leading to his parents' home—though his mind was still back on spending the weekend with Haley and those damn papers.

There was no way all of that was coincidence. He firmly believed she'd left those there for him to find. For one thing, the woman was neat as a pin and everything had a place. No way in hell would she leave papers spread about like that and not in tidy little stacks.

For another thing, she wouldn't leave out confidential work knowing someone outside the company was coming over. She was much more professional and much smarter than that.

Which meant she knew he had a plan. She might not know exactly what his plan was, seeing as how his path had changed a few times, but she knew he wasn't on the up-and-up.

So now what? Did he keep playing this game? Damn it, he hated calling any of this a game. His revenge wasn't a game. His feelings for Haley weren't a game.

But he was too far in to all of this to pull back now. There had to be a way to get the company and the woman. And if Joshua Lowell was truly a stand-up guy, then Chase had to rethink that angle, as well. Josh wanted out, so clearly he wasn't like his old man.

As Chase turned into his parents' subdivision, his mind was already formulating ideas on how, if at all, he could meet up with Josh outside the office. Maybe Chase could tell Josh what he'd found and that would gain Chase more leverage over the competition.

Maybe there was a way to salvage all of this…the revenge and the uncertain relationship he was in.

Thirteen

The warm embrace of his mother always settled his mood for at least that moment. That same familiar body lotion she so loved still took him back to when he was a child and she'd hug him and tell him everything would be alright.

Now he was the one making sure everything would be alright.

Chase eased back. "Is Dad here?"

His mother shook her head. "He's out golfing with some buddies today. I'm so glad you could come by."

She reached around him to close the door, then

turned. "Let's go into the living room. Do you want a drink or anything? I just made some cranberry muffins."

"No, I'm fine."

Chase followed his mother into the living room. He'd purchased this place for his mother once she'd finished her care and while his father was still in prison. The neighborhood was nice and quiet and the spacious home was all on one floor because he wanted easy access to things for his mother.

She took a seat on the sofa and Chase sank into the leather wingback chair across from her. She looked nice today, refreshed with a yellow top and white jeans. She'd pulled her dark hair back into that signature twist she always did.

"You look nice, Mom."

She laughed and narrowed her gaze. "You always said that when you wanted something from me."

Chase shrugged. "That might be true, but there's nothing I need. Can't a son compliment his mother?"

"Hey, at my age, I'll take all the compliments I can get," she laughed.

"I hardly think fifty-eight is old."

She reached over and patted his cheek. "I'm fifty-nine, which you well know, but thanks for that extra boost of confidence."

Chase eased back in the seat and rested his arm on the side. "So, what did you need to see me about?"

"You know I love to visit with you," she told him. "And I hadn't seen you for a few days."

Maybe because he'd been a little preoccupied by the only woman who could ever distract him from his goals and reality.

"Now who's the one who wants something?" he countered. "You texted me to come over and I don't think it was so you could sit and stare at me."

She crossed her legs and lifted one slender shoulder. "Fine. I did want to talk to you not over the phone or text. I want to know what's going on with this revenge you're hell-bent on seeking and I want to know who the woman is who has been keeping all of your time lately."

His once feeble, meek mother had blossomed into a bold woman since her treatment. While he was damn proud of her for overcoming her demons, part of him was terrified. She was still his mother, she still deserved respect and the truth... He just didn't know how much to reveal at this delicate stage.

"I have been seeing a woman named Haley Shaw," he told her.

"And how does she tie in to this whole thing?"

Chase wasn't about to play dumb or insult her intelligence, so he answered honestly.

"She's Josh Lowell's personal assistant."

His mother swore under her breath before letting out a deep sigh. "Don't pull an innocent into this mess, Chase. She couldn't possibly know what happened years ago."

"Actually, she was hired by Vernon while she was still in college," he informed her. "But, I will agree that she is innocent. I started out just flirting, hoping to gain some inside information from her."

"And how has that worked for you?"

That knowing stare she held him with had all of that guilt he'd tried to suppress coming to the surface. He'd never wanted Haley to get so involved in his plot, but he couldn't stop the roller coaster he'd put her on, either.

"Oh no."

Chase pulled his attention back to his mother at her statement.

"What?" he asked.

"You're falling for her."

Shaking his head, Chase shifted in his seat. "I'm not falling for her. We're spending time together, we've gone out. She's an amazing woman. Career oriented and loyal, so that's something I can appreciate."

"You're falling for her," she repeated. "Or maybe you're already in love."

"I have no time or room in my life for love right now," he scoffed.

"Most people aren't looking for it when it happens, son, but you're in deeper than you think. Or maybe you're lying to yourself, I don't know, but if you can't face the truth then someone is going to get hurt."

Like he hadn't already thought of that? Like he wasn't sick thinking of the prospect of Haley getting caught in the crossfire?

Or worse…that she'd hate him forever. Once all of this was over, would she understand where he'd been coming from? Would she believe his feelings for her were real?

Oh, hell. They were real. Now what? Oh, this might not be love like his mother suggested, but there was definitely something more than just sex.

When all of this was over, and he was the CEO of Black Crescent, was there even a chance Haley would listen to him?

"Looks like you have some decisions to make."

His mother's soft tone had Chase easing back in the chair and closing his eyes. These weren't the decisions he wanted to make. He hadn't lied when he'd said he had no time for this, but he was going to have to make time and dig deep to find out where Haley stood. Was she more important than this vendetta or would he have to push her aside to continue his decade-old plan?

"I'd say the interviewing process is about to come to an end. If Ryan Hathaway had taken the job offer, this would've been over weeks ago."

Haley glanced across the large metal and glass desk to Josh. He leaned back in his black leather office chair and seemed quite content this morning. Not typical behavior for a Monday morning, but she was having a great start to her own week. She and Chase had spent the past two days together. They'd made love—could she even use that word at this stage?—and they'd gone to the local coffee shop for mimosas and waffles yesterday morning. They'd watched old movies and shared more details about what made up their personalities. Who knew the man had a secret crazy sock collection?

"Have you decided who you want to take your place?" she asked, crossing her legs and trying not to show her hand or hold her breath.

"I've narrowed it down to three I'd like to talk to again." Josh laced his fingers together and rested his forearms on his desk as he leaned forward. "But I need to talk with you before we move forward with anything else."

She didn't like the tone of his voice or the way he was staring at her like he knew her dirty little secret. Did he know?

So what if he did. Chase wasn't her dirty secret. He was the man she was seriously falling for.

"I've heard a rumor about you and one of the applicants. Chase Hargrove."

Haley inwardly rolled her eyes. Rumor? More like gossip mill. While she truly loved Black Crescent, she also knew this place was like any other office building and one little spark of news always escalated quicker than anything else.

"And what exactly did you hear?"

Because she guaranteed it wasn't near as juicy as what was truly happening, but that was certainly something she'd keep to herself.

Josh glanced down to his hands and blew out a sigh. "Listen, you know you're more than my assistant," he started. "I'm definitely on your side here."

Irritated, she sat up straighter in her seat. "I wasn't aware there were sides."

"There aren't," he amended. "Just listen. I'm not talking to you as your boss, not yet. Right now I want to talk to you as a friend. I've heard you were out with Chase Hargrove. Actually, I heard you were quite cozy while out, which makes me believe there was nothing involving Black Crescent going on between you two."

"I have been out with Chase a few times, yes. He's not an employee."

"No, but he is being interviewed and some might see that as a compromise on your part."

Haley relaxed her shoulders, settling deeper into the seat. She knew Josh wasn't her enemy. Her enemy was all of those negative thoughts inside her mind telling her that she should never have let things go this far, so long as Chase was a contender for the CEO position.

"You should know that Chase is in the top three to take my place," Josh went on. "Would you continue seeing him or do you think you should take a step back?"

Haley wasn't sure what to do. This company literally meant everything to her and Josh was like family. She would continue her loyalty to him and to Black Crescent Hedge Fund…but did that mean she had to put aside her emotions? Did that mean she had to put aside the one personal relationship she'd sought out in years?

"I would never tell you who you can and can't see," Josh went on. "I'm not in any position to tell you what to do. That's all on you. My concern comes from the friend standpoint and I don't want you hurt."

Well, that made two of them. But if Chase

hadn't touched those papers, then surely he wasn't using her…right?

"I want to make sure he isn't trying to get close to you in order to land this position," Josh added. "You're one of the most intelligent people I know, so I'm well aware that you wouldn't purposely let yourself be used. If you tell me you're positive he's on the up-and-up, then I'll believe you."

Haley offered a smile that she hoped was convincing enough for Josh to drop this matter for now. "Chase and I enjoy each other's company. We rarely talk work. In fact, we tend to discuss Tomorrow's Leaders. He's made some generous contributions and…"

The contributions. Damn it. Was he using her? Had she been so foolish, so blindsided by charm and sex appeal that she'd completely fallen for the oldest trick?

"Be careful, Haley."

Josh's concerned tone pulled her from her thoughts. She wasn't about to voice her own opinions or worries here. That was something she needed to sort out on her own.

"I'm careful," she stated as she came to her feet and smoothed down her burgundy pencil dress. "Was there anything else?"

"Should I call him for another interview or would you rather I not?" Josh asked, also standing. "I mean it when I say I want you comfortable with the person who steps into this role."

Not every boss would take that stance. Most people would only choose the person who was most qualified to be in such a leadership position, and no doubt Josh kept all of that in mind, but he also worried about her, which made her sorry he was going to be leaving. She'd been with him so long, she wouldn't know how to come in each and every day and not see his face.

"Are you tearing up?"

Haley blinked, cursing at the burning sensation in the back of her throat. "Shut up."

Josh laughed as he came around his desk and pulled her into his embrace. "If it helps, I'm going to miss you, too. But I promise to stop in. You won't be completely rid of me."

Haley wrapped her arms around him and smiled against his chest. "I'll let you take me to lunch so I can tell you all about the new CEO and we can talk freely."

"I look forward to it." Josh leaned back and stared down at her. "Especially if that person is Chase Hargrove."

Haley didn't say anything. What could she say? Maybe falling so fast, so hard with Chase had been a mistake, considering their positions. Maybe taking a step back for the time being was the wise move to make. Then once the new CEO was decided, whether him or another, then she could revisit a relationship and see where they stood.

But for now, and for the short foreseeable future, she needed to focus on the job and help Black Crescent cross over into a new chapter.

Fourteen

Haley had texted Chase that she needed to speak with him and that she was leaving work around five. Considering that that time was early for her, he had to believe whatever she wanted to discuss was serious.

After their weekend together, he thought they were progressing into something more. But he also had to come to the very real conclusion that she knew that his intentions weren't completely honorable.

None of this should surprise him, though. Haley was a smart woman. She didn't get to where she was by being played for a fool.

Granted there were people, like her disrespecting parents, who saw her only as an assistant. Chase knew full well the value of a loyal, well-trained assistant. They were just as vital in the daily goings-on within the company as the CEO. Just because their faces were behind the scenes didn't make assistants any less esteemed.

Chase pulled into the drive of Haley's cottage home and killed the engine. He wished like hell he knew what he was walking into. How could he formulate a game plan when he didn't have a clue about his opponent?

He cringed at his initial thoughts. This whole ordeal wasn't a game and Haley wasn't an opponent. She'd turned into so much more. At first he'd definitely been using her, but that was just harmless office flirtation. It wasn't until he uncovered her kind heart, her giving nature, the passion within that he realized he was in over his head.

But by then everything had escalated and there was no way he could back out.

There was also no way he could remain in his car mulling over all the ways his detailed plan spiraled out of control. He had to face Haley, but he would say nothing until he knew why she'd called him here. He knew all of this would come out eventually, but he'd hoped his secrets would expose themselves as he took over the company that destroyed his family. Not just his family, but also the lives of several other families in Falling Brook.

Chase stepped from his SUV and readied himself for whatever lay ahead of him. No matter what, he wasn't about to lose everything he'd worked so damn hard for…and that included Haley.

Before he could knock, the door swung wide and she stood before him still wearing her work clothes. Another one of those little dresses that seemed conservative but that drove him absolutely out of his mind. Her hair was down and over one shoulder and her feet were bare.

But that smile was missing. That smile she always greeted him with, that smile that always made him want to scoop her up and escape somewhere, just the two of them, and ignore the rest of the world…that smile that always managed to kick his guilt up another notch.

"Thanks for coming by." She gestured for him to step inside. "I hope you weren't busy."

"Never too busy for you," he assured her.

She closed the door behind him and started toward the open living area. He'd just left here only yesterday, yet the atmosphere seemed so different now. What exactly did she know or did she *think* she knew?

When she didn't take a seat, he knew nothing good was about to happen.

"What's going on, Haley?"

She licked her lips but leveled his gaze. "I've been lying to you."

Well, that was a bold statement to just jump right into and not one he was expecting at all. She was lying to him? There was so much irony in that statement.

"And how have you been lying to me?" he asked.

Haley took a deep breath. "I thought you might not have the purest of intentions when it came to Black Crescent or to me. When you first came in, there was the flirting that I dismissed, but then things progressed."

He waited, listening to her reveal her truth all while he held his darkness deep inside. The guilt gnawed at him, more than he'd ever felt before, but he had to let her continue. He had to let her get this out into the open and off her chest... Then he could see how to proceed and what, if anything, he should reveal.

"Because I'm so protective of Black Crescent and Josh, I did a little digging around on you," she went on. "The attraction and the job became two totally different things and I did struggle with the separation of the two."

That guilt he had suddenly became layered with anger. She had been investigating him? From the beginning?

He had no right to be angry… But damn it, he was.

"Then I uncovered that you had changed your last name," she told him. Her eyes held his as her brows drew in. "I'm not completely certain why you did that, but I have some ideas. There is also the fact that while other applicants sent me flowers and cupcakes, you sent me highlighters and took me out to expensive plays and dinners."

"And those are all strikes against me?" he asked, still irked that she'd had him investigated.

"I couldn't be sure if they were strikes or gold stars," she told him. "I wanted to think someone like you could be attracted to someone like me."

What the hell did that mean? He didn't get a chance to ask before she went on.

"Once you really started showing more interest, I couldn't help but wonder if it was me you were after or the CEO title."

Chase gritted his teeth and crossed his arms over his chest as he continued to listen. She had been second-guessing everything from the start.

She had wondered his intentions from the very beginning and yet she still went out with him… She still slept with him.

"I decided to lay a paper trail to see where your loyalties laid."

That got his attention more than anything.

"You what?" he demanded.

"I'm so sorry," she told him, taking a step closer. "I had to know if you wanted to be with me or if you were really just out for the job."

Fury filled him and he hated himself for so many reasons, but namely for being played from the beginning. He was the one who was supposed to gather all of the information. He was the one who was supposed to make sure his game plan was flawless. But he'd been too occupied with the end result to realize that he'd veered off course of his well-laid plan.

"I know now that you didn't try to deceive me and I just… I had to tell you." She pursed her lips, her gaze continuing to hold his. "I didn't want anything between us because I think there's more here than either of us wanted."

Chase said nothing. What could he say? He was still processing the bomb she'd just dropped. Here he thought he was coming over because she had uncovered his secret, but she had turned the tables and everything he'd known thus far had all been a lie.

She'd questioned him from the beginning, but she'd never outright just asked him. So much sneaking, so many hidden thoughts that were damning to their relationship.

And he was just as guilty, he totally understood that, but he never expected this behavior from Haley. She'd been the bright spot in all of this, she'd been the distraction he'd needed, she'd been the one comfort he'd had because she provided something positive and perfect.

"You deceived me," he accused as the hurt continued to roll through him.

"I did." Haley took another step toward him, then another. "In my defense, I didn't know you well and I had to put my job and the company before any feelings I was developing."

He should've realized that from the beginning. One of the main things that had turned him on about her was that steely businesswoman she seemed to be.

Damn it, he had no right to be angry, but he couldn't help himself. Maybe he was angrier with himself for not seeing what was going on and for letting this happen... Because he had started all of this.

No, Lowell had started this colossal mess when

he'd chosen to interfere with the lives of Black Crescent's clients and then dole out part of the blame before fleeing and leaving everyone else to take the fall.

As Haley stood within reaching distance, Chase realized he wasn't the only bad guy. Here he'd been having guilty feelings, wondering how he could protect her from the fallout when he should have just kept his focus straightforward on his goal and not gotten sidetracked by sex. He never should've tried to incorporate flirting into the mix; that was such a rookie business mistake.

"Say something," she pleaded. "I'm sorry I didn't believe you. I'm sorry I went behind your back, but I'm telling you now hoping we can move on."

But they couldn't move on. While all of this newfound information from Haley threw him for a complete loop, Chase still couldn't give up on his goal.

Which meant he had to give her up. She'd come clean on her actions so they could move forward, but she had no clue that he was still lying. His anger right now stemmed from shock. He never would have guessed she would be playing him right alongside his own game…which just proved how remarkable she truly was.

Damn it, he wished he would've met Haley

under much different circumstances. They would have been a dynamic duo had they teamed up together.

Chase took a step back. Haley's eyes widened as a shroud of sorrow filled her stare.

"I understand your reasoning for what you did," he began, but held his hands out when she started to step forward. "I don't think we should move forward with a relationship."

Haley stared a brief moment before she visibly composed herself. Crossing her arms, widening her stance and tipping her chin up were all indicators she was ready for a fight. But he'd been emotionally knocked for a loop and didn't have the energy right now. He needed to get out of here, to regroup. If that made him a coward, then so be it.

"You're that quick to throw away your feelings?" she asked. "Because I kept secrets to protect my job and my boss? I didn't know you in the beginning, Chase. If the roles were reversed, you would've done the same exact thing."

The roles weren't reversed and he'd done more digging and scoping out the competition than she knew.

"I came clean when I realized I had feelings for you," she went on. "Maybe you don't feel the same, though. Maybe you don't need me anymore now that you had such a great interview and Josh is considering having you in again to talk."

Another shocking revelation, but at the same time, Chase wasn't surprised. He was damn quali-fied for the position…a position that he still wanted and was starting to realize was all he had left.

Circling around to his ultimate goal was where he needed to land. Even though there seemed to be a vise around his heart, he had to remember the reason he'd started all of this to begin with. To seek justice for his family and all of those who didn't have the means to fight back. He had to make this right, and getting wrapped up in an even bigger web of lies with Haley was not the way.

"We both knew this was risky," he told her. "You stated more than once that I could become your boss and then where would we be? It's better to end things now, Haley."

He thought for sure he saw her chin quiver, but her eyes were dry and narrow. She pulled in a deep breath and nodded.

"Fine. I won't beg you to listen to my side and I sure as hell won't ask you to give me another chance. I'm not sorry for the why of all of this, but I am sorry if I hurt you. I would have thought you of all people would understand my justified actions."

Oh, he understood. Which was why he was getting back on track with his plan and putting any unwanted emotions aside.

Haley took a step forward, but she walked around him and went to the front door. He heard the click, but other than that there was complete and utter silence.

Of all the scenarios he imagined of how this would come to blows, Haley opening up about her secrets was sure as hell not one of them. And to add another tally mark to his coward column, he simply couldn't tell her he'd been lying from the start.

That guilt he'd had layered in a messy, sloppy manner with a dose of wounded pride.

Chase turned to face her, but she merely stood there with the door open and stared straight ahead to the wall. He took in her stoic profile and honestly didn't blame her for being angry. Hell, he was plenty angry with himself right now.

At least she was out of the equation for the most part if he could keep her aside. And in keeping her out of the way, he could regain his momentum and control over this takeover and revenge.

Without a word, and without stopping to look at her one last time, Chase made his way to the door and left. He'd barely stepped over the threshold when the door closed ever so softly at his back, but it was that definite click of the lock that was like a slap of reality to the face.

And he had nobody to blame but himself. He also had some serious decisions to make.

Fifteen

Chase loosened his tie and crossed his study to the bar in the corner. Drinking was never the answer, but considering he didn't have the answers, he didn't see how a drink would hurt.

He'd attempted a few online conference calls, but he didn't even care about business today. He'd dodged calls from investors, letting them go to voice mail.

For the past twenty-four hours since he'd walked out of Haley's house, he'd been in a foul mood. Trying to be a professional at this point was beyond even his realm of possibility.

He was still trying to figure out what the hell happened and how he'd missed any clues that Haley didn't believe him.

Chase poured two fingers of scotch and tipped the tumbler back. Slamming the glass back down, he was just about to pour another round when his cell vibrated in his pocket.

He pulled the phone out and glanced at the screen, fully intending to see a work associate, but his father's name popped up.

He might shirk his work for right now, but he'd never purposely ignore his parents.

Chase swiped the screen and answered. "Hey, Dad."

"I hope this isn't a bad time."

Chase stared down into the empty glass. "Perfect timing. What's up?"

"I won't keep you," his father went on. "Your mother said you were here the other day and we've been talking. I need to tell you that it's time to move on."

Chase gripped his phone and stepped away from the bar. He paced the study and ended up at the window behind his desk. The sun had started to set, giving a warm, orange glow across the horizon. The view should be calming, and would be at any other given time, but not today.

"Move on from what?" he asked, knowing exactly what his father was about to lecture him on.

"You're not a fool, Chase. Let this vendetta go," his dad pleaded. "I did my time and Vernon Lowell's sons aren't to blame. They are nothing like their old man. I was guilty of assisting in various acts and you're not mad at me."

Oh, he'd been plenty angry with his father when all of this went down. Chase had been pissed at his dad for putting their entire family's future in jeopardy. But this was the man who had provided and worked hard for their family, so forgiving him was much easier to do for Chase.

"I want that company," Chase stated. "There's no better poetic justice than for me to take over the place that ruined my family."

His father's deep sigh resounded through the phone. "Son, we aren't ruined. We had setbacks, we had a curveball thrown at us, but look us now. Your mother is healthy, and I'm living my life and not dwelling on the past. Let it go. Let it all go."

Chase ground his teeth, listening as his father made sense with each and every word. That didn't mean Chase had to like it. He wanted to get revenge, he wanted to make things right for his family and complete this circle once and for all.

"You need to focus on something else," his father went on. "Or *someone* else."

Of course his parents had discussed Haley, and while Chase would love nothing more than to focus on Haley, she had deceived him…and he had deceived her. What future could they base a relationship off with that kind of start?

And when she found out, she would hate him anyway. Because his deceit was far worse than what she had done. Now that he'd had a little more time to process things, that was the crux of his anger. He couldn't be too upset with her for only looking out for the only type of family she'd truly had. Isn't that what he was doing? Just looking out for family?

He admired the hell out of her because she didn't have to tell him a damn thing…yet she had. She'd been honest and up-front, which was a far cry above where he stood. So if he was going to look down in judgment to anyone, it would have to be himself.

"I know you don't want to hear any of this because you've been determined for so long," his father went on. "But I thought you should at least understand my side. I've moved on and I swear, once you do, you'll find peace and happiness that no revenge could ever bring you. Seeking your own justice will not change the past. Don't let this eat at you any longer."

Chase dropped his head between his shoulders

and closed his eyes. The thoughts swirled around in his mind. A raging storm that continued to pound him over and over.

Could he find peace if he let all of this drop? Could he move on with his life?

For the first time in years, a sprig of hope popped up that had nothing to do with Vernon Lowell or Black Crescent Hedge Fund.

"Haley?"

Blinking away from her computer screen, Haley looked up to see Josh standing at her desk. "Yes?"

"I've said your name three times."

"Really?" she asked. "I didn't hear you."

His dark brows drew in. "I was standing right here and you've been staring at a blank screen for several minutes."

Busted. She'd never been one to daydream at work or get caught in a zombie state.

Haley pushed back and turned her chair to fully face Josh, who still stared down at her like a worried parent.

"Maybe I just need more coffee," she joked.

Unfortunately, Josh knew her too well and wasn't buying her lame attempt to dodge his concern.

"What's going on?" he asked. "You've not been yourself for two days now."

Two days. That was when Chase had walked out of her home after he'd broken things off with her. She'd told him only a portion of what she'd done, what she'd found. She wanted to give him the chance to come clean himself, to tell her anything he wanted to get off his chest.

But he'd ended their relationship using some ridiculous reasoning and he hadn't acted like he was even bothered by letting her go. Perhaps their relationship had been growing on only one side.

"There's no issue if you end up hiring Chase Hargrove. He and I won't be seeing each other in a personal capacity anymore."

Josh glanced over his shoulder to the bustling staff around them. He leaned forward and lowered his voice.

"Are you alright?" Josh asked. "Because I was coming out to tell you he's on his way in."

"Wait." She sat up straighter in her seat. "He's coming here? I don't have him down for an appointment or another interview."

She immediately turned back to her computer and pulled up the schedule, knowing full well Chase's name was nowhere to be found.

"He contacted me directly," Josh stated.

Haley refocused her attention back on her boss.

"That's another reason I came out here," Josh went on. "I figured something was up with the way you've been acting and the fact that he called my direct line, bypassing you completely."

Bypassing her, yeah, that sounded about right with his attitude last she'd seen him.

She couldn't deny that knowing he was on his way sent an unhealthy dose of panic through her. She wasn't ready to face him just yet. She hadn't quite found her emotional footing since he'd ended things.

"Do you want to talk about it?" Josh asked.

Haley smiled. She truly appreciated the way he cared for her, the way he wanted to help that had nothing to do with their working relationship.

"That's sweet of you to offer, but I'm fine," she assured him. "I mean, I'm hurt and angry, but I'll be okay."

The words slid out easily, but she knew actually living up to the promising statement would be much more difficult. And as much as she wanted to get up and head to the break room or anyplace else in this office to avoid seeing Chase again, she would sit right here, hold her head high, and put on the biggest damn smile.

No way would she let him know that inside she had been completely crushed to pieces. How silly was that? How foolish and naive to fall for someone in such a short time? She shouldn't have let herself get so swept away by charming words and a sexy smile, not to mention the way he filled out those damn suits.

And without the suit? That was even more impressive.

"I won't call you a liar, but you're not okay," Josh told her. "Chase should be here in about ten minutes if you want to step away from your desk."

Haley laughed. "You know me better than that."

Josh leaned back and smiled. "Yeah, I do. You're one of the toughest people I know, and for what it's worth, he's a fool."

"Yes, he is," she agreed. "But don't let the personal issues affect what's best for Black Crescent."

"You want me to beat him up for you?" Josh joked.

"Maybe if we were in third grade on the playground I'd take you up on that, but no. I'm going to sit here with a smile and act like nothing happened."

"I expect nothing less."

Josh turned toward his office, but glanced back over his shoulder. "Feel free to make him wait when he gets here. I wouldn't blame you if you want to be a little petty and spiteful."

Haley laughed again. "We'll see how nice I'm feeling once I see how he treats me."

Josh nodded and headed back into his office.

Haley turned back to her blank computer screen and blew out a breath. There was no way she could start a new project and get anything of worth done in the next ten minutes. All she could think of was the moment when Chase would step through the doorway.

Being strong was the only way she would get through this. Her life didn't revolve around Chase or their fling…though what they'd shared had been so much more. He'd cared for her, she knew he did.

But she wasn't going to beg. She had too much going on in her life and she deserved someone who would be there for her as her equal supporter, not someone who required her to ask for the love she desired.

Ugh. Love. Did she love him? After such a short time?

Yes. She did. She loved the guy who took such interest in her charity, who spoke of his own struggles with education and trying to make a better life. She loved how he was witty, charming, commanding and attentive.

Haley closed her eyes and took a deep breath. She was going to have to shove all of those thoughts aside to get through this impromptu meeting. She wondered what Chase needed to discuss with Josh that was of such urgency, but Josh would tell her after Chase left.

She just had to remain calm and plaster that smile on her face to remind him of what he could have had and what he let go.

Sixteen

"I'm withdrawing my name from the list for the CEO position."

Chase stood in front of Josh's desk, wanting to do this in person instead of over the phone or email. Or maybe he'd just wanted to be a masochist and see Haley because two days without her had been too damn long.

"You found something else?" Josh asked as he leaned back in his leather chair.

"No, but at this point in my life, I feel it's best I continue with my global travels and work with startup investors. Black Crescent is a wonderful company, you should take all of the credit for that, but someone else should take over."

Josh's brows dipped in for a split second. "Does this have anything to do with Haley or are you strictly talking from a business standpoint?"

Of course Haley would talk to Josh. They were close, as most coworkers were. When people spent over forty hours a week together, they tended to share everything and lean on each other for some sort of support. Haley considered Josh like her family, so her confiding in him was no surprise. Chase just wondered exactly how much she'd shared.

"Both," Chase answered honestly. "This is the right decision for all of us, trust me."

Though he had to admit, especially to himself, Haley had changed everything in him. His personality, his hatred toward this family, his outlook on the future.

Coming in here and letting go of this vendetta wasn't something he ever would have considered had his father not told him it was time to move on. After all, if his dad could let go, then Chase figured he could, too.

And with Haley in mind, Chase knew it was time to move on with a more positive mindset.

"If this is what you want, then I respect your decision." Josh pushed back in his chair and came to his feet. "But I'm going to offer some unsolicited, extremely unprofessional advice."

Chase nodded. "I assumed you would."

"I don't know the dynamics of what is going on or not going on between you and Haley, but I will say this. You will never find anyone more loyal to have in your corner."

"I'm well aware of how loyal she is," Chase stated.

So loyal she'd gone behind his back and dug up who knew what. But then she'd confessed once her feelings grew deeper…which was more than he could say for himself. He was still stunned at her honesty, but at the same time he was impressed that she'd exposed her secrets.

Everything about Haley touched something deep inside him, something he'd always kept hidden. That little nugget of emotion he didn't want anyone to tap into because he didn't have time for such things…not while he was so hell-bent on revenge.

But his father had said to let it go, and there was one more thing he could do to take things a step further to let all of this hatred go.

Chase slid his hands into his pockets and pulled in a breath. "I need to give you some advice as well and I'm completely overstepping my boundaries here."

Josh jerked slightly. "What's that?"

"It's no secret, the rumors of you having a secret baby."

Josh's jaw clenched, but he said nothing. Yeah, Chase was definitely walking a fine line, but this was pertinent information for Josh to have.

"I have some connections," Chase went on. "The hows and whys aren't important here. What you need to know is the doctor involved in all of this is shady as hell. He's been known to change DNA results for a nice fee."

Josh's lips thinned. "Is that right?"

"There's also a chance your brother Jake is the father," Chase said. "I thought you should know. Do what you want with the information, but if you look deeper into the doctor, that's where you'll find your answers."

Josh blinked, not showing much emotion. "Why did you dig into my past? What's in this for you?"

Chase had resigned from the potential position and he had given up some valid information, but he had hoped to avoid this part. Moving on, though, would consist of coming clean and telling the truth.

"I'm Dale Groveman's son," Chase replied. "My father used to work for yours and ended up going to prison for fraud."

Josh's eyes widened as he circled his desk. "Are

you serious? What the hell were you doing trying to get a job here?"

He stopped, his eyes narrowing as he clearly mentally answered his own question. "You wanted to take over this company for what? To run it into the ground? Destroy it?"

Chase shrugged. "Honestly, I wanted to just prove that I could take it over. I wanted some type of justice, knowing that I was now in charge of the company that nearly tore my family apart."

Josh crossed his arms over his chest, his dark eyes zeroing in on Chase. "What made you change your mind?"

Haley.

"Everything changed since I first sent my résumé," Chase said honestly. "I've learned there's more to life than revenge."

Josh nodded. "There is and it's amazing how a woman can change your entire outlook on life, isn't it?"

Chase wasn't discussing his personal relationship with Haley. He'd come for what he intended and now he was done. There were other places he needed to be, other projects he should be focusing on. Because moving on wasn't just something he was doing regarding Black Crescent. He had to move on from everything that held him here... including Haley.

He'd lied to her, deceived her in ways that were unforgivable. Now that he'd cleared his conscience, he could go.

Ignoring the question, Chase pulled in a deep breath.

"I have the doctor's name who worked on the DNA and the facility he used," Chase stated, circling back to the paternity issue. "I can forward you all of my findings to do with as you wish."

As he took a step back, then another, Chase said, "I can let myself out, and good luck with filling the position and everything else."

Chase had just turned to face the door when Josh's words stopped him.

"Don't be fooled by her smile and strength. She's not like any other woman you'll ever meet, and she's able to handle more than you think."

Chase didn't acknowledge the words, but he completely understood what Josh was saying. Haley would hurt deeply because she loved so deeply. She cared with her whole heart and poured herself into those around her.

Including him.

That guilt he'd been carrying around for weeks seemed to amplify even more since he'd walked out of Haley's home. Chase reached for the knob and opened the door, stepping into Haley's work space.

She didn't even look up from her computer. Her hands flew across the keyboard as she continued right on working. Of course, she knew he was beside her, so she either didn't care or she was purposely ignoring him because of everything. Likely both. He deserved nothing less.

He approached her desk, willing her to look at him, but she never did. Chase stopped beside her desk, noticing a small bouquet of daisies in a vase on the corner. This was a far cry from all of the arrangements she'd had only a few weeks ago.

"Take care of yourself, Haley."

Chase continued toward the elevator without looking back to see if she even glanced up from her screen. He wanted her to have a good life, a great career and a lucrative charity. He'd already contacted his assistant to have more money sent next month, as Chase would be long gone from Falling Brook.

She was rather impressed with herself for getting a good bit of work done for the day. She was trying to compile an informative welcome package to the new CEO...whoever that turned out to be. She wanted them to have a nice, smooth, easy transition.

Having Chase here made her wonder what was

going on, but he'd left hours ago and Josh still hadn't said a word about the meeting.

And it was driving her crazy.

She checked her emails for Tomorrow's Leaders and replied to the ones that couldn't wait. Haley was about to shut down her computer when a message came across the screen for her to come into Josh's office.

Oh, now he wanted to talk after keeping her waiting for so long?

Haley pushed her chair back and moved toward Josh's closed door. Without knocking, she let herself in and found him standing at the window.

"Close the door behind you."

Haley did as directed and slowly crossed the office. "Are you finally going to tell me what that closed door meeting was all about with Chase?"

Josh turned and laughed. "I can't believe you didn't barge in here the minute he was gone and demand answers."

"I'm practicing self-control. How did I do?"

"Remarkably well." Josh smiled and took a seat on his windowsill. "I wanted to wait until the end of the day to talk. I had a few things to get done."

Haley stopped at his desk and crossed her arms. "So what did he want?"

"To withdraw his name from the running for the position of CEO."

"What?" Haley gasped. "He doesn't want the job? But why?"

"He said everything for him had changed," Josh explained. "He said he also had been seeking revenge because his father used to work for mine and his father ended up taking some of the backlash and ended up in prison."

Haley merely nodded.

"You knew?"

"I had him investigated," she told Josh. "I wanted to know more about him for myself, but I also wanted to know why he seemed so persistent. I knew there was more to him than just another billionaire mogul."

Every part of her was shocked that Chase had told Josh everything. He hadn't told her all of his history, but he'd come and revealed himself to Josh.

A good part of her couldn't deny the hurt that hit her hard from that revelation, but another part of her was rather impressed with Chase for owning up to his sins and secrets.

"I don't need to know what went on with the two of you," Josh said, then held up his hands. "I don't want to know. But I think he's a good guy.

Despite the past issues with our fathers, neither one of us is holding grudges anymore."

Haley wasn't sure what to think, what to feel. It had taken everything in her not to turn and look at Chase as he'd left the office earlier. When he'd told her to take care, she'd bitten the inside of her cheek to keep from responding.

"I'm not sure what you want me to do with this information," Haley finally replied. "I mean, he's not going to be working here and we broke things off. You're singing his praises like that's something I need to take with me."

Josh shrugged and shifted in the windowsill to rest easily on one hip. "What you do is up to you," he told her. "I'm just saying, it might be smart of you to reconsider just letting him go. The man obviously loves you."

"Loves me?" Haley asked, shaking her head. "No, he doesn't. He's never said that, never even hinted such a thing."

"Because men have no clue how to express their feelings," he defended. "We're a little dumb in that area, so cut us some slack."

Haley couldn't help but smile, knowing how hard Josh and Sophie had fought to get together. There was something about people falling in love and finding happiness that made them want to play

Cupid with others. That was fine. She was thrilled Josh had found his happily-ever-after and, who knew, maybe one day she would, too.

But she truly didn't believe it would be with Chase. No matter that she couldn't just turn off her switch to these feelings for him, if he didn't want to be with her, then things just weren't meant to be.

"I can see thoughts swirling around in your head."

Josh's words pulled her from those thoughts.

"My mind is always working," she told him. "You know that."

"I know that you're probably thinking more about a man and less about work."

"So what if I am?" she countered with a shrug. "I'll be fine, though. My personal issues won't affect my job."

"I never thought they would, Haley." Josh came to his feet and crossed to her, placing his hands on her shoulders and staring down into her eyes. "Listen to me. If you want to be with Chase, then go. Don't just sit back and let life pass you by."

Haley took in his advice, wondering if she should go to Chase or just let him go. She didn't want to beg, but was going after what you wanted begging?

No. There was no reason she couldn't fight for

what she wanted. She wanted to know what Josh saw that she missed.

Did Chase love her? Well, she didn't know, but she was about to go find out.

Seventeen

Chase laid the stack of dress shirts in the garment bag and hooked the hangers through the top opening. Once they were all in, he zipped up the bag and placed it aside on his bed with his other belongings from the closet.

Turning a full circle around his room, he figured he'd gotten almost everything packed from here and the adjoining bathroom. He didn't have many possessions he just had to take with him. The furniture was of no use and didn't hold sentimental value. So long as he got his personal items, he would be just fine. He could lease this place, rent it, sell it—hell, he really didn't care. His time was up and there was nothing holding him here now. His parents were used to him traveling for business, coming and going as he chose, and he visited them often enough or sometimes flew them to where he was if he knew he'd be gone for a lengthy time setting up new companies.

Once Chase left Falling Brook, he planned on going to his condo in Florida. A little sunshine and beach time would do him good. Maybe that would clear his mind, who knew. He doubted seeing bikini-clad women would wipe his mind of the one he let get away.

Now there was only one thing left to do.

Leaving the old life behind without the black cloud hanging over his head was the only way to push forward. He needed closure and he needed to clear the air with Haley.

The alarm on his front door sounded through the house and Chase pulled his cell from his pocket to access the camera from the front porch.

Haley. Her black-and-white image appeared and his heart instantly clenched at the sight. He wanted to run to the door at the same time as he wanted to ignore her presence. If he hadn't lied to her in such a severe way, he wouldn't be such a coward. All of this guilt and pain had been brought on by him and there was nobody else to blame.

When she'd told him what she'd done by investigating him, he'd been shocked, but all of his anger hadn't been toward her... She'd just been an easy target at the time. No, everything that had gone wrong between them was all on him, and someone so loving and caring and giving as Haley deserved so much better.

How could one person pull out so many emotions, such a mixture of feelings?

He glanced to the screen again, noting her appearance. She still had on her work clothes, her hair left down but tucked behind one ear. Haley glanced toward the camera as if she knew he was looking at her at that precise moment.

His stomach knotted with nerves as his heartbeat kicked up. He shouldn't be surprised she was here after the bomb he'd dropped on Josh. No doubt Josh told Haley everything that went on in the office. He'd planned to see her before he left. A final piece of closure. But he'd been putting it off as long as possible because he was a coward. Now she was here and this was his last chance to make things right.

Chase tapped the button to let her in and he heard the front door open, then close. She was in his home once again and he had to remain calm. As much as he wanted to go to her and beg for forgiveness, he wasn't about to do that. First, he wasn't sure what all she knew, and second, maybe she wasn't here about that. Maybe she wanted him back.

Chase cursed under his breath. Hell no she wouldn't want him back, not if Josh told her what Chase's initial intentions were with Black Crescent.

Maybe she'd come here to tell him off, to berate him for using her... He would deserve nothing less. There was nothing she could say to him that he hadn't already said to himself. He was a total bastard for the way he'd treated her, but damn it, he hadn't expected to get so involved... He hadn't expected his heart to get involved, either.

Realizing he couldn't hide in his master suite forever, Chase stepped from the room and headed down the hall. The moment he crossed into the living room, his eyes met Haley's.

She stood there gripping her handbag, and for the first time since he'd met her, she almost looked nervous. Interesting. If she was here to explode all over him about his actions, she certainly didn't look upset.

"I didn't expect to see you again," he told her honestly.

"I didn't expect to be here again."

As much as he wanted to close this distance between them, Chase remained still. She'd come here for a reason. He just needed to give her the time to process her thoughts and speak or come to him when she was ready.

"So what happened to bring you here?" Chase asked. "You talked to Josh, didn't you?"

Haley stared at him for another minute, then glanced around, her brows drawing in as she spotted one of his suitcases by the sofa.

"Traveling for business?" she asked.

"You could say that."

Her eyes shifted back to him. "You're leaving."

Chase nodded. "I'm done here."

"Because plans didn't go your way?" she asked, a little extra bite in her tone than what he was used to.

"Because I ruined one of the only relationships I've ever cared about and there is no reason for me to stay."

She jerked, obviously surprised by his response. Silence settled heavy between them, but Chase remained still.

Haley took a step closer, then another. She sat her bag down on the sofa, then glanced around the room. Chase didn't know what was going through her mind, but he wished like hell she'd say the reason for her visit because he was going out of his mind with scenarios.

He was also going out of his mind staring at

her and not touching her. That damn black dress hugged each of her curves and he knew full well what each one felt like beneath his touch.

"Your father went to prison for his part in Vernon's scams," she stated, clearly not in the form of a question. "Then your mother battled her own demons."

Haley turned to face him, her eyes holding him in place. "And that left you alone to work through your anger without the guidance and love of those who mattered most."

Chase didn't like how she'd summed up his past in one statement that was so damn accurate. Yes, he'd been hurt, but his revenge hadn't been about his own hatred for Vernon Lowell. Chase had wanted vengeance for tearing his family apart and making them put all the pieces back together.

"Josh told you."

Haley folded her arms over her chest. "I've known for several days, actually. Before I told you that I'd had you investigated, I knew. When I came clean the other day about what I'd done, I was giving you a chance to do the same, but you chose not to. You either didn't trust me enough or you were just continuing to use me."

Wait… She'd known? She'd known about his parents, what had motivated him to start this charade, and she still hadn't told him?

Because she was giving him a chance to speak up in his defense and what had he done? He'd walked out on her. Could he be more of a jerk?

"But Josh didn't act like he already knew when I told him everything," Chase stated.

"That's because I never told him." Haley dropped her arms and sighed. "Don't you get anything? Of course I was going to protect my company had I thought for a minute you would seriously do some damage, but I didn't want to tell him. I'd developed feelings for you and didn't want to betray you."

Something clicked into place at her final statement. The woman who had always put Black Crescent above all else, who'd even stood by their side during the most scandalous time, had put him first. She'd chosen to be loyal to him, to keep his secrets, and he didn't trust her enough to tell her the truth.

Chase pulled in a breath and took a step toward her. "You covered for me."

"I wanted you to tell me the truth," she told him. "I'd hoped if I told you what I'd done, that you'd tell me. So, when you broke things off and said nothing else, I assumed you were only in this to use me for information."

"That's not how it went down."

He took another step, and another, until he'd closed the gap between them. He was close enough to touch her, but Chase clenched his fists at his sides.

"You surprised me when you told me what you'd done," he stated. "I never thought you would have done something like that, but now I realize you were protecting Black Crescent and yourself."

"We do what we can to protect those we love." She offered a sad smile, one that broke his heart. "Before I go, I want to know if you ever had feelings for me, or was all of this just a game to you? Were you only after—"

Chase gripped her face and covered her mouth with his. He couldn't stand not touching her another second. He also couldn't listen to her doubt what they had anymore. Everything they'd shared was real. Everything he felt for her was real.

Now he wanted to show her.

Haley gripped his wrists and opened for him, her passion pouring out of her, and Chase wanted nothing more than to strip her out of this dress and show her exactly how much he'd missed her...how much he needed her.

He eased back slightly, resting his forehead against hers.

"Everything we shared had nothing to do with my plan," he told her. "I started flirting with you thinking I'd get information to use later, but then I lost myself. The flirting turned into a need I couldn't explain and before I knew it, I'd fallen in love with you."

Haley jerked back, her eyes wide. "You love me?"

He hadn't meant to just let that slip out, but yes. He loved her and it felt damn good to have those words out in the open.

The punch to the shoulder was quite unexpected and shocking. She struck before he even saw her move.

"What was that for?" he asked, shrugging his shoulder.

"For putting me through hell, you jerk!" she fired back. "Not only did you deceive me from the beginning, you didn't come clean when I gave you the chance, and now you say you love me? So, what, you were just going to leave town and take those feelings with you?"

"What was I supposed to do?" he countered, staring into her fiery eyes. "I'd screwed up. You deserve someone who's going to be honest and open with you. Someone who's devoted to you, who puts you above all else."

She stepped away from him, propping her hands on her hips. "And you can't be that man? Here all this time I thought there was nothing you couldn't do."

So now she was getting back at him by attacking his pride. That was fine, he deserved her frustration and anger…maybe not the punch, but he'd let that slide. He'd been a complete jerk to her from day one, yet here she stood.

Which likely meant only one thing.

"You love me."

Her brows drew in. "What?"

"You love me," he repeated, reaching for her once again. "I know you do or you wouldn't be here. You wouldn't be so hurt over what I did if you didn't care."

He gripped her hips and pulled her flush against his body.

"And you wouldn't have kept my secret from Josh if you hated me."

Her lips thinned, but she said nothing.

"No denying the truth now?" he asked with a smile.

"I hate you for making me love you."

Chase laughed, knowing he'd won. "That makes no sense, but you're even sexier when you're angry."

Her hands flattened against his chest as her bright eyes held his. She was so damn pretty she stole his breath. And she was his. There was no way he was letting her go again. She'd come here to fight for them, which just proved she was the one for him. He wanted a woman who wouldn't back down. He wanted a woman who understood his mind, his heart. He'd found her.

"You're not moving," she told him. "You're staying in Falling Brook."

Chase smiled. "Yes, ma'am."

She slid her arms up over his shoulders and around to the back of his neck, her fingers threading through his hair. "You're also going to marry me. That family you wanted? I want one, too… with you."

The excitement and anticipation pumped through Chase. He gripped her backside and lifted her body against his.

"Did you just propose?" he asked.

"If that's what you want to call it." She slid her lips over his ever so slightly. "More like I just laid out your life plan."

Chase nipped at her lips as he turned to head toward his bedroom. "Go right ahead and plan my life, so long as you're in every aspect."

She slid her mouth over his, silently answering him. The moment Chase stepped back into his room, he eased Haley down to her feet and went to make quick work on that zipper going up her back.

He peeled that dress off her body, watching as it slid down and puddled at her feet. She kicked it aside, leaving her only in her matching lacy bra and thong and her black heels.

"You're going to be the death of me," he murmured as he reached for her once again.

She laughed as she skirted out of his touch. "Not so fast," she told him. "You have on too many clothes and I don't like the look of this bed with so many bags on it."

He turned, remembering he'd been in the midst of packing when she'd come by. Chase took about two seconds to clear the garment bags off, discarding them onto the floor without a care. There was only one thing he cared about right now and she was standing before him with a desire in her eyes that he wanted to dive into.

Chase kept his gaze on Haley's as he jerked the shirt from his pants and unbuttoned just enough to slide it up and over his head. The rest of his clothes and shoes flew off in quick succession, leaving him completely bare. And the way her heavy-lidded stare raked over his body, he wasn't sure how much longer he could hold back from tossing her onto that bed and showing her just how much he'd missed her over the past few days.

"Now who's wearing too many clothes?" he asked, reaching for her once more.

"Take them off of me," she commanded with a naughty grin.

A blond strand fell over her eye, giving her an

even sexier look. How did he get so lucky to have her come back into his life?

Reaching around her back, Chase flicked the bra clasp. Haley watched him as he removed the straps from her shoulders and down her arms. He flung the garment over his shoulder before moving on to her panties.

He hooked his thumbs in the lacy straps over her hips and eased them down, dropping to his knees as he went. Her hands went to his shoulders and she balanced on one foot, then the other as he removed her thong.

Haley standing there in her heels, staring down at him, might have been the most striking, breathtaking view he'd ever seen.

He trailed his fingertips up her legs, over her knees, inside her thighs and straight to her core. Haley took a wide step as she continued to hold on to his shoulders and watch.

The second he eased one finger inside her, Haley's lids fluttered down as a moan escaped her. Chase held on to her hip with one hand while pleasuring her with the other. In no time, her hips pumped against his hand and Chase couldn't tear his eyes away from the erotic sight.

Haley's nails bit into his bare shoulders as she tossed her head back and cried out her release. Chase waited until her body stopped trembling before easing away and coming to his feet. He wrapped his arms around her and lifted her to carry her over to the bed.

"Tell me again," she muttered as he laid her down. "Tell me you love me."

Chase came over her, resting his elbows beside her head as he grazed his lips across hers. "I love you, Haley. Forever."

Eighteen

"I'm not sure I'm ready for this," Haley stated. "This is quite a step in our relationship."

Chase laughed as he pulled in front of a small cottage and killed the engine. He turned to face her, taking her hands in his.

"It's just my parents, Haley. You're not going before a firing squad."

Nerves danced all through her belly. It had been over a week since she'd gone to Chase's house and told him how she felt. It had been the best eleven days of her life, staying with him, talking of plans for their future.

But parents? What did she know about parent relationships? Hers were nonexistent and Chase knew that. Yet here they were, ready for Sunday afternoon lunch.

"You proposed to me," Chase reminded her. "Did you think you wouldn't meet my parents at some point?"

She glanced down to their adjoining hands and shrugged. "I hadn't thought that far yet. I just knew I wanted to spend my life with you."

He smiled and squeezed her hands. "This is part of my life. My parents are going to love you just like I do."

Haley let out a sigh. Having him say he loved her never got old. She could face anything with him by her side...even parents.

"I'm not good with parents," she whispered. "I don't know how to act or who to be. Are they proper like using the right fork or do I just follow their lead?"

Chase leaned forward and kissed her before easing back. "Honey, this isn't an audition. They already love you because I do. Trust me on this. Just be yourself."

Haley pulled in a shaky breath and nodded. Chase stepped from the car and circled the hood to open her door. He extended his hand and Haley held it tight as they headed up the steps to the cozy front porch with a swaying swing.

Before they could knock, the front door flew open and his mother squealed with delight. His father came up behind her with a wide smile. Haley instantly felt some of the pressure ease off her shoulders.

His mom threw her arms around Chase's neck and kissed his cheek. "I'm so glad you guys are here."

Then she turned her attention to Haley and hugged her, as well. Stunned, Haley returned the gesture and wrapped her arms around Chase's mother.

"You don't even know how excited I am to meet you," she stated, pulling back with a huge smile. "I hope you like chicken and potatoes. I also made a cheesecake with a raspberry glaze."

"Stop fussing," his father insisted. "You're worrying over everything."

Haley instantly found herself relating to this woman. Fussing and worrying over everything was pretty much her job. Haley already felt a kinship to Chase's mother and they hadn't even made it off the porch.

"Come on in," his father said and gestured.

"Lunch is ready. I put everything out on the back patio. It's such a nice day."

Haley followed them through the home and outside to a darling eating area beneath a pergola draped with wisteria.

"Have a seat anywhere," his mother told them. "We aren't formal here."

That was good to know. Haley could tell this place was one of those homes where everyone felt welcome and invited. There was no pressure to be someone you weren't.

Such a far cry from how she'd grown up. No wonder Chase was so giving, so…perfect. He'd had a loving environment and loving support system behind him at all times. Even during the difficult days, he'd had his family.

"Chase tells me you run Tomorrow's Leaders," his mom said as she took a seat across from Haley. "I've heard of that organization and I think it's absolutely wonderful how you're looking out for those kids."

Haley smiled. "I don't do much," she stated. "It's the donors who really make things happen."

"Don't sell yourself short," his mom replied. "If it weren't for you, the donors wouldn't know how to help. An education is so important and there are too many kids who can't afford schooling. Not everyone can get a scholarship."

"That's exactly right," Haley agreed.

The conversation flowed from the charity to Chase's next project, which he informed them was setting up a company in LA to start up their own investment firm. He'd already asked Haley to accompany him, but she wasn't sure if she should leave for vacation in the midst of the new CEO hunt.

Though she doubted Josh would care. Josh seemed to like Chase and Josh totally understood what being in love was like.

"So tell me what my son did to get the attention of someone as wonderful as you," his father said after they'd finished eating.

Haley set her glass of wine back on the table and laughed. "Honestly, it was a bundle of highlighters."

"Highlighters?" his dad asked. "Son, you can do better than that."

Chase laughed and came to his feet. "I completely agree."

He dug into his pocket and pulled out a box. Haley gasped as she stared up at him.

"I know you already asked me to marry you,"

Chase started. "But we haven't made things official."

He opened the box and went down on one knee. Haley stared at the classic emerald-cut diamond ring and tears filled her eyes.

"I wanted to get you something that suited you," he told her. "Something classy, elegant, flawless."

"It's beautiful," she murmured through her tears.

"I want to spend my life with you," he told her. "I want to help you with your charity, I want you to help me grow to be a better man. I want everything, but only with you."

He took the ring from the box and Haley held out her finger. He slid the diamond on and it fit absolutely perfectly. She didn't know how he knew her ring size, but she wasn't about to question it.

Chase came to his feet once again and pulled her up with him. He wrapped her in his arms and kissed her as his mother let out a squeal of delight once again.

"Welcome to the family," his father stated.

Haley turned to see his parents across the table. Both were beaming and Haley realized she was inheriting a family to call her own. Having a man by her side and a loving family was all she'd ever wanted.

Chase wrapped his arm around her waist and Haley realized that she could indeed have it all, and that some things in life were worth fighting for.

* * * * *

Available September 1, 2020

#2755 TRUST FUND FIANCÉ

Texas Cattleman's Club: Rags to Riches • by Naima Simone
When family friend Reagan Sinclair needs a fake fiancé to access her trust fund, businessman Ezekiel Holloway is all in—even when they end up saying "I do"! But this rebellious socialite may tempt him to turn their schemes into something all too real...

#2756 RECKLESS ENVY

Dynasties: Seven Sins • by Joss Wood
Successful CEO Matt Velez never makes the first move...until the woman who got away, Emily Arnott, announces her engagement to his nemesis. Jealousy pushes him closer to her than he's ever been to anyone. Now is it more than envy that fuels his desire?

#2757 ONE WILD TEXAS NIGHT

Return of the Texas Heirs • by Sara Orwig
When a wildfire rages across her property, Claire Blake takes refuge with rancher Jake Reed—despite their families' decades-long feud. Now one hot night follows another. But will the truth behind the feud threaten their star-crossed romance?

#2758 ONCE FORBIDDEN, TWICE TEMPTED

The Sterling Wives • by Karen Booth
Her ex's best friend, Grant Singleton, has always been off-limits, but now Tara Sterling has inherited a stake in his business and must work by his side. Soon, tension becomes attraction...and things escalate fast. But can she forgive the secrets he's been keeping?

#2759 SECRET CRUSH SEDUCTION

The Heirs of Hansol • by Jayci Lee
Tired of her spoiled heiress reputation, designer Adelaide Song organizes a charity fashion show with the help of her brother's best friend, PR whiz Michael Reynolds. When her long-simmering crush ignites into a secret relationship, will family pressure—and Michael's secret—threaten everything?

#2760 THE REBEL'S REDEMPTION

Bad Billionaires • by Kira Sinclair
Billionaire Anderson Stone doesn't deserve Piper Blackburn, especially after serving time in prison for protecting her. But now he's back, still wanting the woman he can't have. Could her faith in him lead to redemption and a chance at love? _____

SPECIAL EXCERPT FROM

DESIRE

Billionaire Anderson Stone doesn't deserve
Piper Blackburn, especially after serving time in prison.
But now he's back, still wanting the woman he can't
have. Could her faith in him lead to redemption
and a chance at love?

Read on for a sneak peek at
The Rebel's Redemption *by Kira Sinclair*

He had no idea what he was doing. But that didn't matter. The millisecond the warmth of her mouth touched his, nothing else mattered.

Like it ever could.

The flat of his palm slapped against the door beside her head. Piper's leg wrapped high across his hip. Her fingers gripped his shoulders, pulling her body tighter against him.

He'd never wanted to devour anything or anyone as much as he wanted Piper.

Her lips parted beneath his, giving him the access he desperately craved. The taste of her, sweet with a dark hint of coffee, flashed through him. And he wanted more.

One taste would never be enough.

That thought was clear, even as everything else in the world faded to nothing. Stone didn't care where they were. Who was close. Or what was going on around them. All that mattered was Piper and the way she was melting against him.

His fingers tangled in her hair. Stone tilted her head so he could get more of her. Their tongues tangled together in a dance that was years late. Her nails curled into his skin, digging in and leaving stinging half-moons. But her tiny breathy pants made the bite insignificant.

He needed more of her.

Reaching between them, Stone began to pop the buttons on her blouse. One, two, three. The backs of his fingers brushed against her silky, soft skin, driving the need inside him higher.

Pulling back, Stone wanted to see her. He'd been fantasizing about this moment for so long. He didn't want to miss a single second of it.

Piper's head dropped back against the wall. She watched him, her gaze pulsing with the same heat burning him from the inside out.

But instead of letting him finish the buttons, her hand curled around his, stopping him.

The tip of her pink tongue swept across her parted lips, plump and swollen from the force of their kiss. Moisture glistened. He leaned forward to swipe his own tongue across her mouth, to taste her once more.

But her softly whispered words stopped him. "Let me go."

Immediately, Stone dropped his hands and took several steps away.

Conflicting needs churned inside him. No part of him would consider pushing when she'd been clear that she didn't want his touch. But the pink flush of passion across her skin and the glitter of need in her eyes… He felt the same echo throbbing deep inside.

"I'm sorry."

"You seem to be saying that a lot, Stone," she murmured.

"I shouldn't have done that." He felt the need to say the words, even though they felt wrong. Everything inside him was screaming that he should have kissed her. Should have done it a hell of a long time ago.

Touching her, tasting her, wanting her was right. The most right thing he'd ever done.

But it wasn't.

Piper deserved so much more than he could ever give her.

Don't miss what happens next in…
The Rebel's Redemption *by Kira Sinclair.*
Available September 2020 wherever
Harlequin Desire books and ebooks are sold.

Harlequin.com

Love Harlequin romance?

DISCOVER.

Be the first to find out about promotions,
news and exclusive content!

Facebook.com/HarlequinBooks

Twitter.com/HarlequinBooks

Instagram.com/HarlequinBooks

Pinterest.com/HarlequinBooks

ReaderService.com

EXPLORE.

Sign up for the Harlequin e-newsletter and
download a free book from any series at
TryHarlequin.com

CONNECT.

Join our Harlequin community to
share your thoughts and connect
with other romance readers!
Facebook.com/groups/HarlequinConnection